Solstice

By

Wendy L. Anderson

Wendy L. Anderson Books, LLC

Cover art by Creation Bound.
Book cover design by Vila Design at viladesign.net
All copyright, title, and interest belong to
Wendy L. Anderson,
Wendy L. Anderson Books, LLC

Paperback: 979-8-9858012-7-9
ePub: 979-8-9858012-6-2

Table of Contents

Prologue

The bonfire crackled, and flames reached toward the sky beseeching the goddess for a fruitful growing season, for love, and fertility. A young warrior stared across the open fire, at the woman who had bewitched his heart. Though he was not her husband, and thus she was not his wife, attraction, need, and desire pulsed strongly between them like the beating of the solstice drums. This was the only night they dared to be together. Other warriors leaped over the bonfire and disappeared into the night chasing after the pale figures of maidens, wives, and even widows. His hair reflected red as the burning coals and hers was white gold like the round moon above. It began, like the sun and moon chasing each other across the skies.

The woman turned slowly and cast a sultry look over her shoulder at him. The warrior stood. She knew the allure of her beauty and took off running into the forest knowing he would give chase. Taking a few steps back, and making a running leap, the warrior easily cleared the flames and landed on the other side. His luck was granted, and without hesitation, he bolted into the woods chasing after the beautiful woman who enticed him to follow. She ran. He chased, with blood pumping through his veins and eyes feverish, his mind aflame with lust. When he caught her there was no hesitation as she turned into his arms. It was new between them and different and frantic. The desire between them would not be denied. She pulled her skirts up and he freed himself, lifted her, and slid into the warmth she offered, and he craved. They both moaned with relief as he began to move inside her, and she clung to him. Their mouths met in crushing kisses as their bodies yearned for the relief they sought in each other's arms.

The magic of the solstice celebration flowed in full force over, through, and around them. The lovers cried out as their fulfillment took them. The gods of fertility sprinkled their blessings over the land and over them.

Chapter One

Graceful stems of heather swayed under the breath of a breeze. The soft swishing sound and delicate movements of the long, thin blossoms rippled over the land like waves flowing in from the sea of rich violet. Runa's footfalls were soft on the rich earth as she pushed her way through the tall lavender-colored bushes. Here in the northern part of Norway, the heather grew thick and extended as far as her eyes could see, all the way to the foot of the blue mountains in the distance where they interspersed with the oak shrub and large boulders. She was almost invisible in the ocean of heather but for her long, loose red hair tossed by the breeze. The faded violet of her dress mixed with the ocean of color, and she ran until she was gasping for air and laughing at her folly. Acting like a young girl was her secret wickedness.

Runa slowed, tilted her face up, and enjoyed the sun beating down on her face as she brushed her hands along the flowering stems. It was an unnaturally warm spring day, and she was free from the confining walls of her village and from the back-breaking work that never seemed to be finished. Escape, even though temporary, allowed her this opportunity to run and pretend that she was still young and happy.

Runa was not married and lamented that she would most likely never find a man. Having reached nineteen winters already, she had no offers for her hand. Her family frequently complained that she was a burden. None of the warriors in the village of Lyngmarker would take her because they did not want to risk her father's displeasure. Sighing, she decided she would not waste the day on such depressing thoughts. Picking a few long stems, she weaved a circle of heather and placed it like a crown on her long, red curls. Resolving to walk just a little farther, Runa went deeper into the fields of heather and walked away from home.

The breeze picked up a little and she stopped. The muffled sound of a moan and then a cough reached her, and she stopped and listened. Her heartbeat raced as fear shot through her. Another moan reached her ears, and she found the direction it came from. She quietly approached, cautiously picking her way through the tall heather. Parting a thick bush, she peered between the branches. Laying propped up against a large boulder, hidden in the thick purple bushes, was a man. If Runa's heart was pounding before, now it was thundering in her chest as her fear turned to terror. Thinking it best, she carefully backed up planning on running away as fast as she could. Runa turned to go.

A fit of coughing took the man's breath away and Runa stopped to listen to the wet choking rattle coming from the man's chest. Compassion took over her fear and against her better judgment, Runa turned back and stepped between the heather stalks facing the man.

The wind shifted and blew his stench toward her. She grimaced. His back was to her and so Runa did not bother to hide her revulsion over the way the man smelled. It was the stench of sweat, dirt, decay, and blood. He remained still as Runa cautiously approached. As she moved around to stand in front of him, she could see that the man was older. Terror struck and she momentarily thought she had come upon one of the *draugr*, the undead. He certainly looked like one with his deathly pallor and large frame. The long beard that fell almost to his chest had once been blonde as had the hair on his head, with dark blonde underneath. Both were now streaked with gray, though he was so dirty it was hard to tell much else about him. His tunic was tattered, his britches were filthy, and his boots were thick with mud. He had nothing but the clothes on his back and, to Runa's alarm, a long sword lying across his thick thighs. The sword looked like the only thing the man took good care of and its sharp blade glittered in the sunlight.

As she approached, a wet cough issued from his wheezing chest once again, and then his eyes flew open. She chided herself for impractical thinking that he was one of the undead as he was most assuredly still alive. The icy menace in his cobalt eyes stopped her movement forward. He weakly raised his sword as if to warn her, but once he saw it was just a girl, he dropped his sword onto his lap again with an audible sigh of relief.

"Help me up, Granddaughter." The man wheezed. "My enemy is not far behind. I must move on."

"My grandfather is dead," Runa spoke loudly incase the old man was hard of hearing. "I knew him and you're not him. Are you one of the *draugr?*"

"Fair enough, Granddaughter. No, I'm not dead…yet." The man garbled and waved a filthy hand at her. "Help me up just the same. The boy is not far behind. I've got to get moving." He leaned to the side and a fit of coughing shook him again.

Runa could see that the man was very ill and feverish, and her heart went out to him. She did have a grandfather once and he had been very dear to her. The sight of this sick old man in front of her asking for help, made Runa feel pity for him. She went and struggled to help him up. Despite his age and affliction, the man was large and powerfully built with sinewy muscles. A wide belt was sinched tight around his flat stomach.

It took some tugging and pulling but Runa finally got the old man to his feet. He towered above her. Dried blood was caked thickly on his right leg, and he favored it as he straightened next to her. He hacked loudly and then spit onto the bushes leaving a line of yellowish-green spittle on the small heather petals. Runa backed away repulsed.

Sheathing his sword, the old man motioned to Runa and rasped, "Where did you come from, Granddaughter?"

Runa hesitated to tell him, but he fixed her with a fierce look out of piercing blue eyes so cold and commanding that the words came stumbling out of her before she could stop them. Her hand rose and she gestured behind her.

"My village of Lyngmarker is that way."

"Give me your shoulder to lean on Granddaughter and take me to your home. I am too sick to go much further. The boy's not far behind and if he catches me, it'll be a swift ignoble end."

"You're sure you're not a *draugr* and you promise not to eat me?" She continued to hesitate.

"No, I'm not dead yet but if you don't help me, I might become a *draugr* and then it would be your fault." He gestured for her to come closer to help him.

Runa hesitated only a second more before a lifetime of discipline and obedience demanded she lend her shoulder to the old man. She had always been a dutiful girl and now that training kicked in and she obeyed.

The fevered heat of his body overwhelmed her, and the smell of sickness was almost too much but she breathed out of her mouth, so the stench was tolerable as they moved forward. He leaned heavily on her and mumbled about *"the enemy"* and *"the boy"* that hunted him. The rattle and wheeze of his breathing mixed with the sound of the wind swaying through the heather.

#

Runa thought they would never reach Lyngmarker. The man was heavy, and they stumbled toward the village with great difficulty. The sounds of dogs barking and children laughing and playing reached them and she breathed a sigh of relief. When the people of Lyngmarker saw her supporting a wounded man, two warriors ran forward and took her burden from her. Without being told to, they helped the man to her father's home. The old man sagged between them, half-conscious.

Runa's father's hold was a longhouse in the center of the village and people gathered around as they took the stranger there. Runa was afraid of her father and what he might say about the stranger she was bringing home. The dogs continued to bark, and the smell of the old man's fevered sweat clung to her. She was distracted by the desire to bathe and change her dress until the heavy doors of the great hall pushed open and out came her father, mother, and three older brothers.

Gorm Haaglanden strode toward the crowd in front of his hall and his curious look found Runa. He scowled at her as he always did. Then his eyes shifted reflecting the familiar look of disappointment he always got when looking upon her. Runa bowed her head, a little ashamed, but then her chin came up slowly as he strode closer. Knowing that showing fear or weakness would make him angrier she bolstered her courage. She had found the old man, and she would tell her father what happened.

"What's the meaning of this?" Gorm demanded, looking around but then his gaze trained on her. "Runa? Who is this man and what have you to do to him?"

"I found him outside the village, in the field to the west. He is wounded and very ill and asked me for help. He said he is being followed by an enemy. I felt I had no choice but to bring him to you and perhaps Mother could mend his wounds. If enemies are coming to Lyngmarker, he may bring warning, and I…" Runa's courage began to waver the lower her father's bushy eyebrows fell and the deeper his frown became. "thought you would want to know." Runa rushed on.

Gorm looked back at the sick old man who hung barely conscious between two burly men and his look softened a little as an indication he really would like to know if enemies were coming. His eyes rested on the huge sword at the man's side and one eyebrow cocked up thoughtfully. The man was unmistakably a warrior.

"Take him inside," Gorm ordered and the men carrying the old man took him into the great hall. He turned his back on Runa and followed them in but then stopped as if suddenly remembering. Turning back, he glared and sneered, stopping her before she could sneak away.

"Runa! You found him; you will help your mother care for him. She has enough work to do."

A small thrill flowed through Runa as she realized she would be there when the old man regained his strength and told his story.

#

A short time later Runa was not so thrilled. After her mother stripped the old man of his filthy clothes, she was called upon to wash them. The stench of the wet rags was so foul that she frequently gagged and had to hold her breath, then turn away to gasp in a breath of fresh air. She wanted to hurry back before the old man woke up so that she could be there when he revealed who he was. Fear was never far from the back of her mind of the enemy the old man mumbled about in his delirium. She gave the clothes a vigorous scrubbing with lye soap scented with heather then rinsed them in water once more and hung them to dry. Then she hurried back inside.

It was growing dark outside, and Runa could not help but look out into the distance toward the towering mountains. A shudder passed through her as if she were feeling the watchful eyes of the unseen enemy that the old man claimed was out there following him. An enemy that his presence there might bring to the village of Lyngmarker.

Runa found her mother examining the old man's wounds when she returned. He lay unconscious upon a straw pallet. The sound of his raspy breathing filled the wooden stall. Runa was grateful for the dim lamp light so that she could watch her mother work and learn by her side.

With a sharp charcoal stick, her mother smeared an ancient rune on his sun-tanned forehead. She sang a charm as she worked calling upon the Asch rune to renew his old strength and so that he would remember his fighting spirit.

While she paid close attention, a moment of admiration for her mother struck Runa as she watched her caring for a stranger. Her willingness to help the sick, injured man was a testament that Mother truly had a good heart. Runa wanted to be like her and display such kindness and care while bringing healing to body and spirit.

The old man was muscular and lean despite his body being riddled with scars, some old and some new. There was a long gash in the man's heavy thigh. Runa's mother ignored that because it had festered so much. She washed his other cuts with water and then applied a thick smelly salve to the wounds and called Runa to help her wrap him with bandages and clean water. When that was done her mother rose, shaking her head in worry.

"He's holding on for now. The leg wound is too far gone, he may lose it or forever walk with a limp. You may try and clean it for all the good it'll do. Watch him until I return and if he awakens, fetch your father immediately." Runa's mother spoke harshly to her, but Runa knew she was preparing her to become a strong woman by being fierce with her. Softness would do the girl no good in such a hard world. Mother left to prepare a healing drought.

The single-bed stall where they put the old man was softly lit by a flickering lamp. Runa wrung the water out of a cloth and wiped his feverish face as she had seen her mother do many times. Though she was careful not to remove the rune. Examining his worn face, Runa again felt the loss of her grandfather and hoped the old man would awaken soon and tell her his story, where he was from, and how he got the terrible leg wound. She listened to the rattle of his breathing and realized, by the wet sound of it, the old man might not live much longer. Wetting the rag again, she did her best to cleanse the bloody gash.

Suddenly, he coughed violently, and Runa jerked the cloth away as his eyes flew open. The old man looked around frantically and one hand patted the bedding as he searched for his sword. As soon as the coughing abated and the old man's eyes found Runa, he calmed. He tried to open his eyes wider and looked around assessing his surroundings.

"Granddaughter?" He looked at Runa while squinting and trying to focus. Runa was pleased he remembered her.

"You are in my home. Rest, you are very ill and badly wounded."

"The boy!" The old man rasped.

"What boy? There was no one with you when I found you."

"He's coming…not far behind…I must be going."

"You are too sick to go anywhere, and your leg is too badly wounded to support you. Stay here for now, my father and brothers will protect you from your enemy."

The old man tried to sit up, moaned in pain, and then fell back. Glancing at Runa he saw the sad compassionate look on her face, and he tried to smile.

"Don't worry Granddaughter, it will take more than a bad cough and a scratch on the leg to kill me. I'll be ready for the boy when he comes." He laid back and stared upwards. His red cheeks glistened with sweat.

"I'll get my father."

Runa raced out of the room to fetch Gorm. He came straight away with Vidar her oldest brother. They crowded into the entrance of the small stall where the old man now lay awake. His breathing rattled wetly in his broad chest. Gorm moved in and settled his great bulk on a low stool while Vidar stood tall and imposing in the entryway with one hand resting on his sword hilt and the other hand slowly stroking his lush beard.

Vanity was not usually a man's trait, but Vidar was overly proud of his thick silky, dark gold beard. It was his habit to caress it with his long, thick fingers. Runa thought it made him look as if he was thinking about important things all the time. The sound of her father's deep voice brought her attention back to the old man and she tried to pay attention.

"I am Gorm Haaglanden. I am Jarl of Lyngmarker. This is my eldest son, Vidar. Tell us what enemy follows you? How many?"

"The boy! He is a day, maybe two behind me." The old man sucked air into his lungs and his cheeks puffed out as he stifled a cough. He was delirious.

"A boy? How many others are with him?"

"No, just the boy, but don't let him fool you. He's got giant's blood in his veins! He's cunning, fast, and deadly! A berserker, protected by Surtr himself! He won't rest until we're all dead. I am the last. I must keep moving or he will catch me too. The boy is coming!"

Runa shook with fear. If this boy the old man spoke of was truly a giant, protected by a fire demon who ruled the fiery wilderness in Muspelheim, then her village was truly in grave danger. She had brought this trouble upon them by bringing the wounded man here.

The old man worked himself into a fit of coughing. Runa's mother came in with a horn cup filled with a healing draught. The small stall was crowded, and Runa had to step out to allow her mother access to the sick man. Runa could hear her father continue questioning the old man but soon he had lost the strength to answer and Gorm grew frustrated. He and Vidar finally left. Runa followed him out into the main room of the great hall that was the gathering place for the men of Lyngmarker. The room was full of curious onlookers and women who wanted to leach a bit of gossip from the men's talk. Runa stayed in the shadows and tried to listen as Gorm addressed everyone.

"The old man's not right in the head. He says he's being followed by a boy, but that the boy is alone. I could not get much more out of him than that. He didn't say where he came from or what his name is, but I don't think there is any danger from one boy. We'll get more information once the old man is well enough to speak clearly. Until then, close the gates and have the lookouts be wary."

Murmurs of assent rose, and the people turned and disbursed back to their daily tasks. Runa hid in the shadows trying to avoid her father's notice, but as always, he seemed to find her out.

"Runa!"

He yelled, bringing her out of her hiding place behind one of the main posts that supported the roof of the hall. Runa eased her way out into the open. She kept her hands behind her and gripped the intricate carvings of the post as if holding on for dear life.

"Don't think I don't know you snuck away again! I'll deal with that later, for now, you have work to do."

"My chores were done Father, and I just left for a moment to gather some heather!"

She started to defend herself, but the look on her father's face warned her and, in the end, Runa just nodded her head and tried not to look afraid. She knew what "deal with that later" meant for her. Already she could almost feel the lash across her shoulders, or his hand stinging her bare backside. The humiliation a beating always brought made her cheeks burn red and the way Gorm's hand lingered on her stinging flesh made her very uncomfortable. The temptation to run through the vast heather fields outside the village was always too great to resist and it was worth the lash. Maybe this time, the beating would not be too bad.

Chapter Two

Runa stayed by the old man's side all night. She washed his feet and hands. The thigh wound was a terrible gash where the flesh had been laid bare from a sword stroke and was filled with dried blood and dirt. The wound should have been stitched closed but had been allowed to heal open for too long. The old man had tried to wrap it with a dirty cloth, but now it was swollen, red, and smelled putrid. Using a rag, Runa scoured the bad wound again. She was determined to clean it so that it would heal better, and he would not lose the leg entirely. Scrubbing vigorously was all she could think of doing. She rubbed away the dried blood and dirt, dipping the rag frequently into the wooden bowl filled with warm water and dried herbs. It wept pus and fresh blood as she worked. She scraped off some of the dead skin with a sharp knife and then slathered on some of the wound salve and wrapped it tight. Runa wanted to do her best so that her mother would be pleased with her. As Mother said, if the old man did not lose the leg altogether, he would more than likely have a limp and a nasty scar for the rest of his days.

Runa thought of her mother Signe, a tall, slender, golden-haired woman. Her striking beauty was known throughout the land, and she was also known for her talents as a healer. She married Gorm when she was fifteen and together, they had three sons Vidar, Bjorn, and

Vonn. Runa was the youngest, the only daughter. Gorm never wanted a girl child but here Runa was, and he barely tolerated her. Anything that made Gorm unhappy made Signe unhappy, so instead of loving Runa as she did her sons, Signe treated Runa as if she were something to be ashamed of. When it was obvious that Runa would not grow to be a golden beauty like her mother, Signe resigned herself to teaching her only daughter to be a healer so that she could benefit Lyngmarker in some way.

Once, when she was younger, Runa overheard her mother speaking to one of the other women. That was when she learned the truth about her birth. One solstice festival, Signe had gone into the forest with a man who was not her husband, Gorm. It was Flynn Bloodhead, Gorm's biggest rival, and a hated enemy. She described her moments with Flynn when they were deep in the forest that solstice night. Signe had taken the opportunity of the celebration to lay with another man despite Gorm's warning her against it. The minute he disappeared into the forest with another woman, Signe had singled out Flynn Bloodhead and led him to a moonlit glen. There Flynn took her under the solstice moon when the goddess of fertility walked among lovers. During the telling of the tale, Signe's eyes grew distant with magical memories as she described what happened on that distant solstice night. Her face had taken on a wistful stillness and Runa remembered her mother smiling, which was rare. As she told of Flynn's fine form, the gentle way he touched her, and pleased her, her eyes filled with tears as memories overtook her. Nine moons later, Runa had been born with a head full of red hair and Flynn's fine features.

No one ever said anything about the children conceived during solstice festivities, but everyone knew. Gorm had golden hair as did all his sons, as did Signe. It was clear, Runa was not his, but rather from the seed of his enemy, Flynn Bloodhead. Thus, she was made to pay for her mother's actions and Gorm hated her. He treated her like one of his thralls.

When she was alone, Runa often relived the moment when she heard her mother's hard, unemotional declaration to the other woman, "Runa is Flynn's, a solstice child."

Often, as Runa recalled that story and the soft look on Signe's face, she wondered if her mother loved Flynn. If she did, then why did she seem to hate Runa so much? Perhaps it was because Runa was a reminder of what Signe could not have. It was the mystery of Runa's life and the source of her unhappiness, but she was determined to earn her mother's love by becoming a great healer.

She let the rag plop back into the bowl of dirty water as her mind jerked back to the present. Runa dried her hands and looked up to find the old man staring at her. His eyes looked less feverish but in the dim lamp light, it was hard to tell.

"You're awake." She smiled.

"A beautiful smile you have, Granddaughter." The old man took a deep breath as if talking and breathing were difficult at the same time.

"I see you are still delirious! My smile is not beautiful! I've been reminded of that every day of my life."

"Nonsense! You are just coming into your beauty. Mark my words, Granddaughter, you will be the envy of all other girls in a year or two."

"Stop talking, you'll start coughing again and *I'll* be in trouble for the noise. All the lies coming from your mouth will give you foul breath." Smiling, Runa admonished the old man.

Embarrassed by his praise she looked down at her hands. They were red and chapped from washing clothes all day and from tending the old man. She shrugged and hummed the same tune she heard her mother singing earlier.

He lay silent for a few minutes and his breathing was slow and loose. Runa finally left him and went to fetch him some broth and bread. When she returned, he was still awake and watched as she brought the bowl closer. Balancing the bowl, bread, and a flagon of ale she set it down on the floor next to the box bed before helping him sit up a bit and handing him the bowl. The old man's nostrils flared as he smelled the heavy beef broth and his lips twitched in anticipation of the meal, but his hand reached toward the flagon of ale first which he drank deep.

Stopping to catch his breath, he wiped his mouth with the back of his shaking hand. Drops of ale dribbled through his gray-streaked beard. Drinking the broth next, he tore a chunk of the dark course bread off and dipped it in.

Runa watched the old man eat and listened to his labored breathing as he tried to breathe through his mouth and eat at the same time.

"What's your name?" Runa ventured. "Where do you come from?"

"My name is Eiland Biersson. I come from nowhere. My village was burned to the ground many years ago by..." He hesitated, stopped eating, and stared into old memories before continuing but set his jaw firm and said the words slightly hushed, "the boy!"

"What boy? You keep speaking of him. Why are you afraid of one boy?" Runa's hands were once again in her lap, and she twisted a lock of her red hair that hung long, resting across her legs. It was a nervous habit, and she hardly knew she did it. Watching the old man with great interest she let herself enjoy the attention he was giving her. He looked her in the eye as he spoke and did not.dismiss her right out of hand or revile her.

"It's a long story." Eiland Biersson began slowly but then fell silent. He ate quickly like a man who was not used to such good food. He looked down into his bowl and scraped up the remains of his broth with the last of his bread. Then he drained the ale and held his empty cup toward Runa, waiting for her to refill it.

Runa left, filled a flagon, and returned quickly, hoping against all hope that the old man would tell her more of his story. After the old man drank half the ale, he seemed a bit revived and turned his blue gaze on Runa.

"As most young men trying to make their way up in the world by searching for riches, I went raiding with the men of my village. Trying to make our fortune, we pillaged churches and small villages. We sailed the long boats across the seas and took what we wanted. After many a raid, I returned to my home victorious and provided my people with the spoils of my deeds. Then one day about ten years ago, my ship was blown off course by a terrible spring storm. Many men were ripped overboard by the hands of Njǫror and pulled down into the crashing waves."

As Eiland spoke of Njǫror, the Norse god of the sea. He held his large hands up and swiped at the air as if mimicking the violent waters ripping men from the boat.

"Thor beat the skies above with his hammer Mjolnir, splitting the black clouds with thunder and brightening the gray seas with flashing lightning. It was an unnatural storm like none of us had ever seen before as if the gods were fighting overhead and we were just in the way. Many of my brothers perished in the violent gray seas of that storm. All of us that were left, eventually hit land as Thor's fury died out. Of the seventy men on the ship, there were only twenty left alive when we finally reached the safety of northern Jutland. When morning came, we saw where we were stranded and that our ship was badly damaged. Up the coast a bit, we found a farmstead built of stone and strong timber. There were sheep and some cows, I don't remember everything. I do remember we saw an opportunity to loot and take what we could, but we were sick and injured. The family there was not much of a threat to us. We told them if they would feed us and let us rest there, they would not suffer any harm from us as we were too weary and sick from fighting the storm. Though I knew that some of the men would never keep that promise. The farmer's wife was comely, golden, and robust, with big breasts and wide enticing hips. The husband was more of a farmer than a warrior with two young sons. Then there was, *'the boy'!*"

Eiland stopped speaking and shuddered. His eyes were unfocused, staring back into the past. Runa saw his pale face frozen in a trance as if he were experiencing a vision, as he relived the tale he told. Compassion filled her and she slid her hand in his as he spoke.

"Large, he was, for only being about ten winters old. He had strange, light blue eyes and looked at us as if he could read straight into our treacherous hearts." Eiland swallowed loudly.

"The farmer's woman fed us, and we rested from fighting the storm. Then the farmer helped repair our boat. It took a couple of months. The boy seemed to lurk everywhere! Watching us, taking note of each face, each name, looking at us as if he knew he couldn't trust us. At least, that is what I thought at first."

Eiland stopped to catch his breath after all the talking and then downed more ale. He held his cup out to Runa asking for more. She quickly filled it and returned it to him and silently waited for him to continue his tale.

"After a few weeks, on the last night, we had regained our strength. The ship was almost ready to set sail, and you have to understand it was our nature to take what we wanted. It is the way of things with warriors set on earning a reputation and gathering wealth. Dursi started all the troublemaking for the farmer's wife. He always was one to go after the women. The farmer left to help stock the ship with provisions so we could leave on the morning tide. While he was down by the ship, Dursi dragged the woman to the back room to have his way with her. He was humping away when the boy found him.

Dursi didn't have a chance; the boy had a knife and then all Hel broke loose. My men didn't take kindly to one of our own being killed and they looted and torched the house and killed the farmer and his family before escaping. Some men took off after the boy to kill him too, but he escaped. The last thing I remember…I saw him standing on a hill. The flames from his house made his whole-body glow red and his eyes were large and white like a demon's eyes. You see, he made a deal with Surtr the fire demon for protection and became unstoppable. He shouted down as we dragged our plunder back to our ship, that he had marked us all and vengeance would be his!"

Eiland shuddered and drank more ale. He was silent as the memory let him go and sat for so long that Runa thought he might be asleep. Then he took a deep, shuddering breath and continued his story, with a voice hushed by fear.

"For the next ten years, he hunted and slaughtered everyone in that crew, one by one. With an unnatural skill, he's found us all. At first, we thought we outnumbered him and could take him, and we fought back, but the boy is as fast as Thor's lightning and cunning as the trickster, Loki. He followed us back to our village and struck us when we were sleeping, working, or taking a piss by the side of the road. We found old Alfred in the woods behind his house. The boy had sliced open his belly as he sat on a log taking a shit. We fought back of course, and got close to catching him a few times, but he'd always slip away. Finally, we split up and left the lands we knew, running from the boy. The others died one by one over the years and sure enough, all of us that had been on that voyage when we killed the boy's family, died by his hand. Now, I am the last of that cursed crew and the demon-boy is coming for *me!*"

Eiland's words died, and his head slumped down on his chest. The breath in his lungs rattled loudly and he slept as if retelling the tale had completely drained him. Runa took his cup from his loose fingers, pulled the wool blanket up to his shoulders, and left him to his dreams.

As promised, the next day Runa's father remembered her indiscretions from the previous day and dealt with her in his usual fashion, repeated slaps across her bare backside. Signe had warned Gorm frequently not to strike Runa's face and make her any uglier. Runa bore her punishment in silence as she knew crying out only seemed to make him strike harder. When she kept still and concentrated on taking her mind to another place to avoid the pain, she could tolerate the stinging blows a little better. When Gorm finished with her, Runa gingerly went about her chores and continued to tend to Eiland Biersson. The thought of *the boy* was always in the back of her mind.

Chapter Three

A week later, early on a sunny afternoon, Signe summoned Runa. She instructed her to take a basket and go out to the forest and collect more of the herbs and plants they used in their healing draughts and salves. Runa was filled with joy over the task and complied happily. Since this was an outing sanctioned by her mother, Runa would not be beaten for going out into the fields and forest. Enough time passed since her last beating and the bruises were mostly healed and she was relieved.

Skipping through the fields and into the heavy forest, she rejoiced in her freedom once again, but quickly chastised herself to remain on task or she would not find everything her mother asked for. The damp smell of dark earth, the whisper of the forest's breath, and the crunch of the leaves welcomed her.

Since the day she found Eiland Biersson, Runa had been the one to tend him. She was more than pleased with that as it allowed her to practice her skills as a healer. The plants she gathered today would bring him healing and her mother might be pleased with her. The man, she came to admire. He slept most of the time, but when he was awake, his eyes glittered brightly, and he told her stories and old legends. Most of the stories were about the boy he claimed was not human and said that he would follow Eiland to the ends of the earth. Rumor spread and the people in Lyngmarker began to think the old man was mostly crazy, so disregarded his claims that he was being followed by a *boy* who had so far, hunted and killed nineteen seasoned warriors.

Eiland was kind to Runa, and she secretly began to care for him in her heart. He was grateful for her care and company, and was the only one who ever called her, *"beautiful."* Runa dreamed of leaving the village of Lyngmarker, seeing the wide world, and escaping her cruel family. She wanted to head off to adventures in the wide world. The only thing she would miss was the heather fields that offered her so much solace in her cruel world. Getting Eiland well and on his feet became the plan and she hoped when the time came, he would take her with him.

Runa's foraging took her deeper into the woods that flanked the heather fields and Runa came upon some mushrooms. These were Gorm's favorites and, though it would not garner any kindness from him, she gathered them anyway. If his temper toward her was lessened for even one night, Runa would be happy.

Not far off, she spotted *another* mushroom growing in the damp shade. Its red spotted caps atop white stems were unmistakable. If eaten in the right quantity that mushroom would cause severe stomach pain, loosen a man's bowels, and make him vomit violently. In larger quantities, it could cause death. Runa stared hard into those shadows where the poisonous mushrooms grew and thought about putting those in Gorm's stew. After a few moments, she shook her head, chastised herself, and remembered she was supposed to be learning to be a healer, not a murderer, even if Gorm deserved it.

She knelt in the black dirt and carefully picked the harmless mushrooms and placed them in her basket. Lost in her task, she hummed a tune to herself and daydreamed about escaping with Eiland Biersson to places beyond her hard life. She would take her skills as a healer and go out into the world saving the sick and healing the wounded.

Eiland also told her tales of Freyja, the goddess of love, beauty, fertility, and war who possessed the magic of foretelling the future. Though she had heard many of these tales since she was a young girl, Eiland had a way with words and his retelling was always better. His eyes glittered with wonder as he spoke of famous warrior women called *"shield maidens"* who went to battle fighting alongside the men. Briefly, Runa fantasized about training as a shield maiden and becoming one of the mighty warrior women. Her thoughts were filled with flashing silver swords, streaking arrows, and glorious battles. Somehow, she would become like Freya or become one of the shield maidens and travel the world away from loneliness, back-breaking work, and the cruelty of her family.

Her daydreaming distracted her so much that Runa did not hear the sound of someone sneaking up on her. Gooseflesh rose on her arms and her breath caught as the cold metal of a knife blade suddenly rested against her throat. Runa dropped what she was holding, and her dirt-covered hands froze in midair. A man's arm snaked under her arms, across her chest and she was yanked to her feet.

"Where is your village, girl?" The hot breath of a man blew against her ear as he spoke in a low, growling voice. The man pulled her against him and held her so tight she could not draw breath.

"Ah," Runa's tongue cleaved to the top of her mouth in fear and that was all she managed to get out.

"Tell me now before I slit your throat!"

Runa raised her free arm a little and pointed in the direction of Lyngmarker. She could not think, her body shook as terror took over her thoughts. The blade lifted a little and her body was swung around and slammed against a tree. A thick muscular arm pressed her back. The very rough tree bark pricked through her worn dress and the pain from being crushed against the tree caused her eyes to water. Blinking away her tears and holding back her fear, Runa glared at her captor. Embarrassment stung her cheeks as she berated herself, *'some warrior woman you would make!'*

The man was tall and wide in his shoulders. Dirty blonde hair hung tangled down to his tunic collar, and he glared at her out of ice blue eyes, the eyes of a killer. She could not make out much of his face through her blurry tears, but she could smell that he had not bathed in many days. The smell made her eyes water even more. She struggled against the arm holding her and tried to bolt away. If she could get a head start, she could warn her village of the enemy warrior. That is when she remembered the boy Eiland had spoken of and she wondered if he had finally arrived. Although it was not a boy who held her against the tree, it was most definitely a *man*.

Blinking away her tears, Runa raised her chin and looked at the hard lines of his features. He was not ugly, but his nose had been broken once. A thin scar ran from his eyebrow to his temple and disappeared into his hairline. Underneath all the dirt it was hard to tell his age, but he was young as his facial hair was pale on his cheeks. His eyes were old and knowing, showing years of painful memories. Most impressive was his armor, heavy leather, polished black, and decorated abundantly with silver, it spanned his impressive chest. A long sword was sheathed at his side, and he held a dagger in the hand pushing against Runa's throat. It did not appear that his strength was taxed at all while he easily held her against the tree.

He made no move to release her after she pointed the way to the village, but instead, he reached down and grabbed her wrist with his free large hand. Turning in the direction of Lyngmarker, he began to pull her along without another word.

Runa dug her heels into the dirt and pulled back, trying to yank her wrist free.

"Wait! My basket! I have to take it back to my mother or she will beat me."

The stranger stopped and gave her a surprised look. Then his eyes searched the ground and he saw the basket. Some of the contents had spilled on the ground in their scuffle. He seemed to consider for a moment while Runa struggled against him. Her mother would be furious with her for losing the basket and not returning with the herbs and plants Runa was supposed to collect. Also, Eiland needed some of the herbs she had gathered. At the moment she was not sure who she was more afraid of, her mother or the stranger. It was that fear that made her panic and pull even harder reaching toward the basket. The man let her wrist go and Runa flew backward and fell hard onto the ground with an indignant "Uff!"

"You cannot outrun me so don't even try. Take me to your village, and you won't be harmed."

Runa scrambled to her knees, cast him a glare, and began to collect the spilled items from her basket. The mushrooms had been crushed by the man's big feet when he grabbed her. Mumbling curses under her breath, she felt even more of a fool as she had landed on a rock and her hip was surely bruised.

Taking her time, she thought about how to get away and what it would mean to the village of Lyngmarker if she took this warrior there. Then again there were many men in the village, and they could stand up to one attacker. The thoughts running through her head quickly sobered her and took her mind away from hurt and embarrassment and centered on one course of action and that was to *'run!'* As soon as her basket was filled and secured, she slowly got up, clutched it to her chest, and bolted.

Runa was slim and lithe, and she was fast. Her long legs pumped as she sprinted away from the man. Through the trees and around bushes she ran as fast as she could. Risking a look behind, she saw he was right on her heels and her eyes widened in fear. Strangely, he had a slight grin on his face as if he were enjoying the chase. Runa scowled and looked forward, paying attention to where she was running. Red braid flying behind her she used one hand to hold her skirts up and the other to secure her basket. The sound of his pounding footfalls catching up to her beat the ground in time with her heart pounding painfully in her chest and her breathing was reduced to desperate gasps.

Moments later he caught her. They fell in a pile of twisting limbs and flailing arms. Weak and out of breath, she struck out but only succeeded in landing a blow on his shoulder. Tossing her around like she weighed nothing, he rolled on top of her and pinned her body to the dirty ground. Runa cried out trying to throw him off, but he was heavy, and the silver-plates of his armor dug into her ribs. He looked unimpressed with her efforts, so she stopped struggling. Both of her wrists were pinned by his massive hands above her head. Gasping to catch her breath, she went still beneath him. As soon as she felt his body relax, she brought her knee up as hard as she could and delt a satisfying blow to the softness between his legs. His face when red and he gave a pained grunt but did not get off her.

"Be still!" He shouted in her face as he pressed her down and squeezed her wrists painfully.

After a few moments of crushing her, when she finally stopped trying to fight him, he pulled her to her feet. Runa was a little satisfied to see him slightly red-faced and breathless from her knee strike, but it did not last.

"I guess I would have been disappointed if you had not tried to run."

"My father will kill me if I bring a stranger into the village!" Runa spat at the man who turned and pulled her along.

"Tell me," he ignored her, "have you seen a wounded old man come through here in the last few days?"

She realized this was the *boy* who had been chasing the old man she found wounded in the heather. The old man who now rested comfortably in her father's longhouse. Falling silent she refused to divulge anything.

As a warrior, the man was trained to notice everything about his enemies, and he looked closely at the girl. She had thick, long hair the color of red autumn leaves. When he tackled her to the ground and she struggled against him, he felt rounded breasts and a slim, almost boney, figure. Her eyes were sparkling blue, and she was attractive despite her worn dress and dirty hands. He had surveyed her small backside as she knelt in the dirt grabbing her things. On the ground when he lay atop her, his agitation stirred in a different direction. The blow from her knee had cooled that instantly. Resisting the urge to grab her again, the warrior crossed his arms over his chest and watched for her to make another attempt to run. He was not worried; he would only catch her again. When she finally bent to retrieve the basket, she slipped it over her arm, his eyes trailed over her full lips and angry set mouth.

"Answer my question, girl. Has a stranger, an old man, recently come to your village?"

He waited, almost holding his breath. The man he chased, was the last one, and once dead, he could rest, then…he would see what fate the Norns had weaved for him.

"My father will kill me if I reveal anything to you!" The girl brushed past him walking in the direction she earlier pointed out. "He'll beat me for taking an enemy there and then my mother will beat me for not getting everything she asked for. Your big feet crushed the plants she wanted, and I'll be blamed for it."

"It sounds as if you are beaten a lot. Are you such a rebellious daughter against your father and mother that you deserve such treatment?" He tried not to sound interested, instead, he stared at the girl's swaying hips in front of him.

"It's none of your concern," Runa said petulantly.

Behind her, the warrior smiled at her attempt to be feisty with him. His prey, it seemed, was within his grasp, and he needed to focus. Even though the girl had not revealed it, she had stiffened when he asked, and given away by her body language that the old man truly was in the village. Now the girl seemed resigned to her fate and trudged on. When the sight of the village walls rose in the distance, he reached out and grabbed the girl's shoulder. She stopped and her back stiffened in fear. The warrior unwound a rope he had coiled at his side and made a noose. He carefully slipped it over the girl's head and in a completely strange act, carefully plucked a few twigs and leaves from her hair. Runa looked up at the warrior tying her up and wondered why he was doing this. She had not tried to escape or run, well, after the first time, and he had ample opportunity to tie her up before, so why now? The village walls were just in sight, maybe he expected her to make a run for it again and call for the thanes within to protect her. She was surprised when he spoke softly with a hint of interest in his voice.

"What is your name?" He asked as he pulled her wrists together and tied them loosely with the rest of the length of rope. The bindings were so loose she could easily slip out of them, and she frowned. The basket still hung from her elbow with the remaining contents safe inside.

"Runa Gormsdotter, what's yours?" She tried to sound defiant but the fear of the beating that awaited her made her voice quiver.

He did not answer, only stared down at her for a moment. *'By the gods, she is beautiful!'* he realized, but then sobered, his brows pulled together, as he gave her an angry look.

"I won't be here long enough for my name to matter. Perhaps I'll reveal it later for the Skalds to craft a poem to honor my great deeds, but for now, you don't need to know." He finished binding her and then drew his sword and shoved her forward.

Runa trudged toward the village as if she were approaching her doom. The sharp end of the warrior's sword hovered at her back. She hoped that she looked enough like this warrior's prisoner and not like she had helped him. It was only the truth, she hadn't really, but if she could avoid another beating for something that was not her fault, it would be a boon. Then again, had she been paying attention and not dreaming of glorious deeds and training as a shield maiden, she might have noticed an enemy warrior sneaking up on her.

'Some shield maiden you would be.' She repeated to herself, as the tall fortifications of her village drew closer.

Chapter Four

The guard on the wall saw them approaching and shouted for reinforcements. Runa looked up and saw as men scrambled along the walls and took their defensive posts. Spear tips pointed down as Runa and her captor stood in front of the closed gates. Looking up she spotted the familiar face of her oldest brother, Vidar. Closing her eyes, she took a deep breath and embraced her fate. He would never open the gates simply for Runa's sake. Behind her, she heard the warrior inhaling deeply before shouting up to the top of the wall. She could not look and only bowed her head in defeat. Surely, she would die now with all her dreams unfulfilled.

"Open the gates! I've your clan's woman as a hostage. I am looking for an old man who came to your village a week past. Send him out and I'll release the girl in exchange!"

"Keep her, she's a pain in the arse! And we don't bargain with fools." Vidar shouted.

"You'd so easily consign one of your women to death!" The warrior sounded surprised.

"I said, we don't care about her! She is no better than a thrall! A stupid girl who allowed herself to be caught by an enemy, she deserves to get what is coming to her." Vidar leaned over the wall and smiled.

"Who is this man who cares so little about his clanswoman?" The warrior spoke quietly to Runa.

Her head was bowed, but she recognized the sound of the speaker's voice.

"He is Vidar, my brother," Runa said flatly.

"Huh," he grunted before yelling up at the gates again. "Send out the old man or I'll butcher the girl right here and you'll be known as a kin slayer. I'll start with one limb at a time, and you can listen to her screams for hours. Then I'll burn your village to the ground and kill everyone in my way until I get the old man. He is nothing to you so send him out and spare me the trouble!"

Runa shivered and began to struggle until the warrior placed his blade against her throat and held her tightly. It must have been enough of a threat to make the men of her village give in because the gates creaked, and the wood groaned. They slowly opened and twenty men stood on the other side, with swords drawn and shields hefted ready for battle against one lone soldier who was brave enough to threaten an entire village.

"Move, girl." The angry warrior ordered.

Striding forward, Runa did not raise her head to look at her kinsmen. She was relieved that the warrior was not going to get the opportunity to butcher her but still felt as if she were walking toward her execution. Surrounded by Lyngmarker's soldiers, Runa led the man to the center of the village where her home was. They approached the longhouse. The ornate rune-carved doors opened, and her father walked out of the shadows of the hall. Her mother was close behind. Runa looked up into their faces. Gorm was frowning as usual, and her mother looked curious. Signe raised an eyebrow at her and pursed her lips as if to ask, *"what trouble have you gotten yourself into this time?"* Runa bowed her head realizing she failed her mother, yet again.

"Don't say a word." The warrior warned quietly, and the sound of his voice grated against her nerves. She shuddered and huddled into herself berating herself for her foolishness while she tried not to cry.

"Send out the old man who came to your village recently and I will release your kinswoman." The warrior shouted bravely despite the number of warriors standing against him. Runa's father looked impressed, but it was only fleeting.

"If you don't, I'll butcher her in front of you and her screams will haunt you to the afterlife."

Gorm crossed his arms over his chest and stared down at Runa and her captor. A strange look flickered across his face, then hardened. Many details were suddenly apparent to Gorm. One that his daughter was tied and held at sword point by the stranger he had been warned about. A warning he mostly ignored. The second was that his daughter had revealed that the man was indeed in the village and brought the threat to his door. Runa looked up and stared at her father who glared at her. The warrior behind her, she knew from tales that the old man told, was a berserker with the protection of a fire giant and had the skill to kill many men before being killed. She would be caught in the battle and slain first, bound as she was, she would only be meat to be trampled in the mud. Looking at her mother, her eyes pleaded for help. Signe just scowled then her eyes traveled over Runa's shoulder and her features softened.

A crowd gathered around them, and Runa felt the eyes of the village people on her. Her mother was staring into the crowd with her lips parted slightly and her brow furrowed. It was a look Runa was familiar with and that is how she knew Flynn Bloodhead must be standing behind them. Runa gave a subtle sigh of relief knowing her mother would not let Runa be slain in front of him, her blood father. Whatever happened now, Runa knew she would live through this.

"I'll take on this young wolf."

Flynn Bloodhead's voice boomed out behind them, and Runa felt the warrior grab her and spin around to face a new threat. She saw Flynn and gave him a grateful half-smile. The warrior grunted as if he immediately saw the resemblance between his captive and the new challenger. He instantly figured out that

Runa was another man's child and not the child of the man she called father and who was the village chieftain, the Jarl.

This large redhaired man was flanked by other redheaded thanes.

"I can take one or all of you, I don't care, but vengeance is within my grasp, and I grow impatient. Send out the coward! Now!" Runa flinched as he shouted above her ear.

Gorm turned red in the face. He would not be embarrassed by Flynn Bloodhead championing his daughter if he wouldn't, even though he knew she was not his flesh and blood. There was more at stake here than just Runa's life and he'd be damned if he'd lose face in front of Flynn and the rest of the village. It would be better to show cunning and wisdom in front of his people.

"If it is a fight you want…a fight you shall have but let us avoid spilling the blood of *my* only daughter. Release her and tell us who you are and why you want the old man. There is no glory in killing the sick and wounded."

"There is a blood feud between him and me. I am on a quest to collect a blood debt. The old man is the only one left, the last I need to finish taking my revenge against or die trying. If I have to cut through you and your men to do it, I will! Send him out, put a sword in his hand, and let me finish this."

Just then the doors behind Gorm swung open and out stumbled the old man. He was clutching a blanket around his shoulders and his feet were bare. Spittle dribbled from his mouth and his eyes were glazed, his face red with fever. The warrior had been holding Runa's arm and at the sight of the old man, he swung her behind him and shoved her into Flynn Bloodhead's arms. He must have known exactly where Flynn was standing because Runa was caught by her champion and was now safe. Flynn held her tightly against him and whispered something that Runa could not hear as shouting and cursing had begun.

Runa saw Flynn look down and slip a finger in between the loose bindings and test them. Slowly, looking her in the eyes, he raised an eyebrow. He stifled a grin as he figured out that she could have sipped the ties at any moment. Runa quickly looked away blushing that she had been found out.

Standing, legs spread in a battle stance with sword drawn, the warrior shouted for the old man to come forward and meet him. Stumbling into Runa's brothers who stood beside Gorm, the old man flailed his arms and tried to utter a war cry. Instead, he tripped down the two stairs of the hall, fell to one knee, sticking out his bandaged leg and catching himself with a loud moan of pain. He coughed until his face was red and he could not draw breath. The warrior looked at him with disgust but did not step forward to take the old man's head just yet.

"Wait! You don't want to kill a sick old man." The old man rasped between coughs. "I'm tired of running from you, *draugr!* Give me time to regain my strength. Meet me on even ground, hale and whole and I'll give you the fight your heart desires. Let my lungs clear and my leg heal then you can try and take your vengeance. I warn you though, do not harm any one of these people who have been good to me in my last days. One week and my sword will be ready for you."

Runa could not see the warrior's face, but his shoulders were tight, and his back was straight. His chest heaved with anger, and he looked every bit of what his foe called him, a *draugr,* a demon. His vengeance was close at hand and yet the fight was still denied to him. He gripped his sword so tight that his knuckles were white, and he trembled with rage. She wondered if he would turn into a berserker in front of their eyes and slaughter everyone.

Gorm shifted. He must have spotted an opportunity to appear magnanimous and prove what a wise leader he was because a smile spread across his face. Taking charge, he raised his arms, pushed his chest out, and stepped forward. Motioning behind him and gesturing for his sons to help the old man stand. They moved forward to do as their father bid.

"This old man speaks bravely. My wife has been treating his wounds and sickness and can attest to his injuries, but tomorrow starts the summer solstice festival. It is a celebration of love and fertility and is a time we worship the gods and goddesses, as is their due. It is not a time for killing. We will have peace for the twelve days of the solstice festival. By then the old man will be well enough to stand and hold his sword, you may fight him then. There will be no killing today or until the end of the festival. Accept these terms and you will be welcome in my hall as a guest. Until then, come eat, drink, rest, and celebrate with us. I warn you though, I have a feeling this old man will not be as easy to kill as you think."

Signe opened her arms and stepped forward to stand beside her husband. Her eyes did not rest on the stranger, but over his shoulder where Flynn Bloodhead stood beside Runa.

"Please be welcome in our home. Come celebrate the summer solstice with us. Surely, the goddess will smile upon you for honoring her with peace and patience."

The warrior had no choice but to comply because fighting during the solstice festival was forbidden even where he was from. Striking down a sickly old man was not something his warrior's code would allow, and the summer solstice was here, so he had no choice. He waited a few minutes considering his choices. In the end, it was the promise of battle that would satisfy the blood quest and give him the pleasure of killing his enemy in a glorious, final fight.

"You, Gorm Haaglanden, will make a *heitstrenging* with me. Give me your solemn oath that I will fight my enemy and I will agree. Peace until the twelve days of the solstice festival is over, then the old man is mine. That will be your promise to me, and you better pray to the gods they do not take him in his sick bed before I have my revenge. My vengeance is at hand and there will be bloodshed to pay the blood debt one way or the other."

"As you wish. You have my promise." Gorm nodded and gestured back to the hall, "Come inside and taste my wife's mead. I'll wager it is the best you've ever had. We'll drink on the agreement and officially begin celebrating the summer solstice." Gorm offered the invitation with a smile.

"I'll not step one foot under the same roof as houses my enemy."

The sound of the warrior's voice was less than appeased. Gorm slowly frowned. He did not take the rejection well.

Flynn Bloodhead stepped beside the stranger and spoke loudly so that everyone could hear him.

"He can share my roof for the duration of the celebration. My wife's mead is as good as Signe's and no enemy sleeps within."

Though he had first offered to fight to defend Runa it was clear that the warrior had not meant her harm. The offer was made to get the upper hand over the Jarl. Flynn and Gorm stared hard at each other across the space where everyone watched in tense silence.

The old man was being helped back into Gorm's longhouse and the men stopped to watch what was happening. All eyes were on the warrior and only Runa was watching Grandfather carefully. He was staring at the boy with deep hatred, and she saw a cunning look pass over his face and the limp lessen as he straightened and walked back into the hall. Either he was faking being as sick as he appeared or had some other motive, but he fooled the boy into thinking he was much sicker than he was and thus put off the inevitable fight.

The warrior turned and drew Runa's eyes away from the old man walking into the hall. Her bonds had been cut and she looked no worse from his rough treatment. She gave him a fleeting, relieved look. The warrior nodded once, and he followed Flynn toward the opposite end of the village.

"Runa!" the sharp feminine voice of her mother screeched out and Runa's face paled. Clutching her basket, she hurried past the warrior with her head bowed and her shoulders hunched. As he followed Flynn, he stopped to look back and saw the girl running up the steps, her mother cuffed her on the side of the head as they went in and the doors to the hall banged shut.

Chapter Five

Flynn Bloodhead led the stranger through the village to his hall. People gathered around to stare at the newcomer. Flynn's house was almost as large and grand as Gorm's. The walls were sturdy and intricate carvings decorated every wood pillar, door, and beam. The people there seemed happy and at ease. Flynn's men were not threatening. The fire was burning brightly, and the smell of roasting venison filled the air. Many flickering lamps were evenly spaced throughout giving the impression of great wealth that oil was not used sparingly. The hall was homey, warm, and comfortable. Flynn went to sit in a large chair covered with pelts and gestured for the warrior to sit beside him. First, the stranger looked around, taking note of the exits, how many women and children were within, and how many armed warriors were there.

"Sit Stranger. I am bound by the laws of hospitality to assure your comfort as well as your safety." Flynn Bloodhead waved again to the fur-covered chair next to his where the man could sit in a place of honor.

This earned him a scowl, and though the stranger finally sat, he was far from relaxed. His body was tense and coiled to leap up at the slightest provocation. The hilt of the sword at his side was always within reach of his hand.

"What is your name, warrior?" Flynn asked as an attractive woman approached carrying a pitcher and two horn cups.

She flipped her red braid at the stranger after banging the pitcher onto the table as if peeved to have an extra man to wait on. Pouring a golden liquid into each cup she handed one to her husband and the second to the stranger, then stalked off shaking her head.

"I am Brand Keitelsson." He accepted the cup but did not drink until after his host did.

Flynn noticed the stranger's hesitation and with obvious movements drank deep and wiped his mouth with the back of his hand.

"People call me, Flynn Bloodhead. Welcome to my home." They raised their cups to each other, and both drank.

Brand could see where he got the name "Bloodhead" because the man had a head full of dark red hair and a full beard of the same color. Before Flynn could ask more questions or begin a friendly conversation, he leaned forward and looked his host in the eye, speaking first.

"Why is a daughter of yours living with another family and calling another man father? The girl who led me to the village, Runa, is obviously your daughter and not that of Jarl Gorm Haaglanden."

Brand was not sure what made him ask this question first. Perhaps he could not forget her sad face as she walked toward her family home, or the smack from her mother when she was within reach.

Flynn Bloodhead poured more ale into their cups while staring down, shame colored his face, but he remained silent. The same woman who brought the mead was returning with a platter piled with meat, goat cheese, and bread. She placed it before the men with a frown. Flynn watched her with cool blue eyes as she tended to the meal. He did not start speaking until the woman left again. It was clear he was waiting for her to get out of earshot.

"I don't mind telling you the tale." Flynn began as he reached for some bread. "It is true, Runa is my daughter. She is a Solstice Child. Her mother Signe, our Jarl's wife, and I went into the forest…as people tend to do during the summer solstice festival. We lay together that night and nine moons later, Runa was born with red hair and features like mine. It could not be denied that she was of my seed. Solstice children are usually loved and accepted as gifts from the gods, but not poor Runa. I have always been the biggest contender to be Jarl of Lyngmarker against Gorm. When Gorm found out Signe and I had been together at the solstice, he was enraged and swore eternal hatred toward me and the girl. To spite me, Gorm claimed her as *his* daughter and there was nothing I could do about it. Gorm dislikes Runa because I slept with his wife…" Flynn stopped and gave Brand a huge grin, "and he hates me because I am his rival."

Flynn stopped to take a bite of meat and then went on as he piled his trencher with more food.

"Gorm likes having something of mine under his control. Consequently, everyone in his hall hates her because I fathered her. Signe refused to give me the girl even though I offered many times to acknowledge her as my daughter and raise her under my roof. Even though they mistreat her, there is nothing much I can do for her if Gorm claims her. He's not fooling anyone because everyone knows Runa is my blood. I protect her when I can. I had hoped when she came of age, Runa would be able to leave Gorm's hall, marry and finally find some happiness. But none of the men in the village will have her because they fear risking the Jarl's displeasure. My sons are her brothers, so it would not be right to pair her with one of them. The other women under Gorm's roof don't like her because she brought Signe such unhappiness."

"It is not the girl's fault her mother lifted her skirts to a man who was not her husband." Brand frowned.

It grated on his personal code of honor that Flynn was dallying with a married woman, but he had never loved anyone and could not understand much of the relationship between a man and a woman. A vision of Runa running from him in the forest made him shift in his chair uncomfortably.

"That is true, but life is hard, and the girl will have to find her way. She is stronger than she believes. Her time will come."

Flynn took more of the bread and cheese from the platter and then pushed it toward Brand. He dished up a hardy amount and began to eat. Between mouthfuls, Flynn spoke on though he lowered his voice and leaned closer.

"Signe has bewitched me. Every solstice she calls me into the woods while Gorm is off with another woman. Every time, I jump over the bonfire and follow. My wife serves me well enough, but she longs to be a Jarl's wife and can make my life difficult with her ambition and greed for riches. Signe is the one in my heart and is hard to say no to." Flynn spoke between bites. "Now, tell me your story Brand. I am interested in why you want to kill that sick old man."

Brand continued to eat and remained stubbornly silent. It wasn't until he finished and drank two more horns of mead that he sat back and began to tell his tale.

"I was little more than ten winters old when raiders came to our home. They did not come brandishing swords and waving torches. No, they came under the pretense of friendship asking for help. Their longship was washed up on a nearby shore. They were sick and wounded, needing shelter. The ship needed repairs before it could be seaworthy again. My father was a craftsman as well as a farmer and offered to help. How could he not with twenty sea-soaked men at the door? Our land gave abundantly, the surrounding woods were full of game, and we had much to share and offered the crew our hospitality. It took a little over a month to repair their ship. We fed them and my mother cared for the sick and wounded. The night before they were to leave one of the crew decided my mother should give more than hospitality, food, and shelter. When she refused, he took what she wouldn't willingly give. I caught him and I killed him. The rest of the men didn't like that, and in retaliation, they killed my father and my brothers and burned our farm to the ground. To my shame, I was the only one to escape alive. I swore vengeance upon every man on that ship. I had learned enough about where they came from to hunt them down. I was only a boy when I set out, so I used cunning and stealth to kill them one by one. That is also when I discovered I could call the berserker in me. It has been ten years since that night. Ten years I've hunted and killed them all…except for one. The old man I saved for the last because his betrayal was the most grievous. Once he is dead by my hand my family will finally be avenged."

Flynn stroked his red beard thoughtfully and drank his mead, considering Brand's words carefully. After pouring more to drink, he leaned forward and looked at the warrior with understanding, but his voice was full of disapproval when he spoke.

"Norsemen go raiding for fortune and to earn their names in battle. The reputation they gain is all a warrior can leave of himself before going to Valhalla. In lean times, they prey on those more fortunate and even those less fortunate. It is the way of things. There is not a warrior among us who has not gone a Viking up the river taking what they can find and bringing spoils home. Much of the wealth in this village has been looted. We've killed our fair share, burned homes, farms, and even churches, and taken castles and hostages as thralls. We have even been raided a few times and defended our homes and families from men just like us. Many women in our village were taken in raids from other lands. My mother, a flame-haired chieftain's daughter, and many women from her tribe were stolen from a place called Eire. The strong take from the weak and sometimes the weak learn to become stronger to survive. We prevail because we are better at fighting and more cunning in battle. Why is it you cannot understand that this is the way of a Norseman's life? Why must you waste your youth on revenge? You should be glad the gods spared you and not squander your life wallowing in hatred and seeking vengeance."

"They came under the guise of friendship." Brand raised his voice. "They ate our food, drank our ale, slept under our roof, and enjoyed our hospitality. My mother treated their sickness, set their broken bones, and sewed their wounds! *I* sat at their feet, listening to their stories every night while they were planning their deceit and murder. I learned their names and had dreams of being a strong warrior like *them* one day. But when I saw that man forcing himself on my mother who had been so kind to them…a blood fever took over my mind. All I could see was red. All I could think of was killing the man who hurt my mother and his friends who killed my family! Can you not understand the depths of that betrayal? I still hear my mother's screams in my dreams! Now, the last man from among those traitors will fall to my sword. It is my duty to avenge my family, or I will die dishonored, unworthy to eat in Odin's hall when I die."

Chapter Six

Gossip spread throughout the village and Runa learned that the warrior's name was Brand Keitelsson. She had listened intently to him when he spoke to her father making his demands. As for Eiland Biersson, it was unclear if he was afraid of the warrior he called, *"the boy."* He was partially resigned to his fate, but his eyes held a glint of cunning.

He was silent later that night when Runa brought him dinner. His cough was better, and his fever was gone, the leg was healing. The Asch rune to renew his strength had served him well. Now the coal marking was fading as if sinking into the old man's sun-browned forehead, giving him its magic. Head bowed and eyes averted, Runa handed him a bowl of stew and a thick piece of bread.

"Granddaughter, do you think me a coward because I wouldn't fight the boy today? Why won't you look me in the eye?" Eiland took the offered bowl.

"No, I just...*I* brought that warrior here. He caught me in the forest, held a knife to my throat, and made me bring him. Now, after the twelve days of solstice festival, he will kill you."

"You had no choice, Granddaughter. I hold no ill will against you." He hesitated, "Did he hurt you? When you were alone in the forest, did he..."

"NO! he did no harm. He bound me and made me bring him to the village. That's all. I was daydreaming and let myself get caught."

"I am sorry I have brought this berserker to your village. You stay away from him Granddaughter. He is a fiend! A demon! He has no soul just a desire to burn, kill and destroy. I will fight him and maybe I will lose, but I will die with my sword in my hand, and I'll sit with my brothers feasting in Valhalla. It will be a good death."

They sat together and Runa listened to the old man tell new stories as he ate his dinner. Something had been bothering her about earlier, of him coming out of the hall to confront the stranger. Finally, she looked up and spoke her mind.

"Grandfather, you…when you came out of the hall, you seemed very frail and sickly, but I know, because I have tended you…your wounds are almost healed, and your sickness is better than you *pretended* to be today."

The old man smiled at her, and his face was transformed, looking almost handsome. He tilted his head toward her and his eyes sparked with mischief.

"You're a very clever girl. There is no dishonor in what I did. I simply let the boy think I was very ill and not much of a threat to him. I did it to throw him off his guard. If he thinks he kills a sick, wounded man, there is no honor in that. *If* I misrepresented how ill I am…" he shrugged, "it will be to my advantage. The boy will find out soon enough that I will not go to Valhalla easily. I'll fight him and I will win even though he is young and strong, I am more cunning and experienced. I'll kill the boy, do not fear for me, Granddaughter."

He took her hand, his eyes begging for understanding. His warm, dry skin was comfortable clasping hers as they stared at each other. A strange feeling passed between them, and Runa swallowed nervously. Gorm walked in and saw the two holding hands leaning close together. He looked from Eiland to Runa and back again with narrowed eyes. Runa quickly pulled her hand away while looking embarrassed and dismissed herself. Brushing past him, Gorm's thoughtful stare followed her as she left.

#

It was the morning of the first day of the solstice festival and Runa woke with excitement flowing through her veins. She was determined that this was the year she would dance with the other maidens around the pole and maybe even catch the eye of one of the village men. If she could find a husband, she would be free from her father's beatings, her mother's slapping hand, and her brother's berating and insults. Her plan was simple. After her chores were finished and she tended to Eiland Biersson, she would sneak away and wash and prepare her body for the celebration to come. This was Freya's day and Runa felt the magic in the air.

The twelve-day celebration would consist of days of feasting, sacrifices to the gods, games, competitions, harvesting, planting, and endless drinking. Tonight, called Freya's night, a huge bonfire would be lit to begin the solstice celebration. It was to be a full moon and surely the goddess would bless the whole village with plentiful crops and fertility for their livestock. The maidens would dance around a pole signifying Freya's spear. In white dresses, with wildflowers threaded through their hair, the first dance would mark their passage to womanhood. The ceremonial drums would pound the fever-lust into the young men. When the moon was highest in the sky, the maidens would let themselves be chased into the forest and caught. The lovers would embrace under the watchful eyes of the goddess who brought abundance and fertility to the land and the people of the village. Hopefully, as the young men and women paired off, future marriages would be secured, and alliances formed. Runa was sure she would find a husband on this magical night.

A slight ripple of fear struck her between the shoulder blades. She knew that it was on a night like this that her mother had gone into the forest with Flynn Bloodhead. They had lain together even though they were each given in marriage to other people. For the solstice festival, the acts committed were overlooked in the spirit of the celebration. Runa was the unloved result of one such solstice joining. A ripple of sadness passed straight through to her bones. She had not bothered to ask if she was allowed to participate in this evening's celebration as she knew Gorm did not want her to. Since she had come of age, she had asked each year and received the same answer, so this time, she did not bother. Tonight, she might be rejected by every man, or she could be caught by an old man, or a married man or no one would jump over the bonfire for her. There were many things that could go wrong. There were also many things that could go right. By tomorrow morning, she might be betrothed, *if* everything went as she hoped.

The people of Lyngmarker were in a festive mood that morning. The women bustled everywhere preparing the meat and bread, mead, and ale for the celebration supper. The day was busy and went very quickly. Runa gathered and helped prepare the herbs they used to flavor the meat and food. She hauled buckets of water, ran errands, and helped her mother bathe. She brushed out Signe's long golden hair and braided it skillfully. When a final strand of beads was placed over her mother's head and the last silver bracelet clasped onto her arm, Runa stood and gazed at her beauty.

"Mother! You are so beautiful! Everyone will admire you!"

Signe looked at Runa in her worn dress with water and stains spilled down the front of her, sweat causing her unruly red hair to stick to her brow. Her hands were chapped and red from the bath, cheeks red from the heat, and Signe frowned and then scowled at her. Lifting her daughter's chin with one finger, she tilted her head side to side and looked her over. With a touch of sadness in her eyes and a flare of red in Signe's cheeks, she whispered.

"You look so much like your father."

Runa tried to decipher if it were regret or longing tainting her mother's words. Or did she lament that Runa was not more like her? Turning away, she sighed heavily while Runa waited for her mother to reveal more, but she did not, she only snapped at her.

"Runa, you stink. Go to the river and wash then come back and help the other women serve the meal at the festival."

With that, Runa escaped. She stopped briefly in the small stall where she slept and gathered her bathing implements and a clean shift along with her best pale blue tunic. The soap and lotions she helped her mother make would leave her smelling sweet and make her red hair gleam. Hope filled her breast, surely, she would find a husband tonight. Slipping away, she headed into the forest.

Her bath was quick and purposeful in the cold waters of the river. Her red locks looked darker red when wet and she used a bone comb to sort through the tangles, letting it dry as she sat on a small blanket in the sun. The trees whispered in the slight breeze around her as she slipped into a white underdress. Thinking of dancing around the pole on Freya's night, and smiling at a handsome warrior, the face of Brand Keitelsson rose unbidden in her thoughts. The stranger had strong features, bright blue eyes, and dark gold hair. It was clear he had been on the road for a long time and the sun had bronzed his skin. When he grabbed her, his hands were firm, but not hurtful and when he pulled her against him, she felt the ripple of muscle banding his arms. Thinking back on it now, she found it tantalizing. She swallowed, feeling bad that she had such thoughts about an enemy. He was a berserker, a *draugr* and the only feelings they possessed were to destroy, kill and maim, but there was something about this one.

Tilting her face to the warm sun, she thought of bonfires and warriors lusting for maidens. She thought of the runes Gebo and Wunjo which meant love, gifts, and joy and she hoped they would rule her day and her night.

Before bed last night, with some stolen thread, she sewed those runes on the inside of her maiden's under-shift. She wove them into the corded belt worn over her ceremonial dress with spiral designs and would take those as talismans to the solstice feast tonight. If the goddess was listening to her entreaty, tomorrow she would no longer be a maiden and a new life of love and joy would be the gift she would receive. Her desire to become a shield maiden rose strong within her breast again, but Runa pushed it away. She must face reality and instead embrace a different dream, that of becoming a wife and mother. Brand the berserker would kill Eiland Biersson and leave, and Runa's life would go on as it always had within the village. The only certainty in her life was that there was no hope of ever escaping. The next twelve days of the solstice festival would be her only opportunity to escape the cruelty of her mother's home, and Gorm's disdain. Starting a life of her own was her greatest wish and her only hope. She must find a husband to protect her from Gorm. Hopefully, she would find someone to go into the forest with tonight and he would end up as her mate. They would spend the next twelve days getting to know each other at the games, wrestling matches, sacrifices, and feasts.

The faces of many of the eligible warriors flitted through her mind. There was Baird, Oskar, Emil, and Geer, but none of them set her pulse alight. She thought if she flirted with one or two during the supper, and they showed interest, she might be able to like one. Though, they would need to like her enough to risk Gorm's displeasure.

There was always Gorm to contend with, but after the deed was done, he could do nothing to stop her. Then there would be ways of staying away from her mother and him once she was married. Perhaps, someone in Flynn Bloodhead's household would choose her. She dreamed of living in his home as she was his blood, and he was the father of her heart. Happiness could be within her grasp. No other face rose to the surface of her daydreaming, but the stranger's did.

Her thoughts were distracted by rustling in the bushes. Listening intently, Runa heard the sound of the flowing river past the bank where she lay warming in the sun. Birds chirruped overhead and so she dismissed what she thought was her imagination. The breeze gave her a chill and gooseflesh rose on her arms. She felt a presence then and realized she was not alone. The stranger, Brand Keitelsson, stepped out of the bushes and suddenly stood in front of her.

Brand was very much altered from the last time she saw him. He no longer wore his armor, only his sword. Bare-chested, standing in clean britches, his hair was damp from washing, and his face, body, and hands were clean. Having bathed, slept, and eaten, he lost the gaunt, hungry look he had when he first took her captive. Now, he looked younger and far less threatening.

Approaching her slowly, his eyes wandered down her form as if he could see right through her thin dress. The flicker of interest in his blue gaze was a surprise to her. Runa found herself intrigued and enticed by him.

Unfastening his sword, he slowly approached, placed it on the ground, and sat next to her without asking permission. Together, they stared forward at the river, each seemingly lost in their thoughts. He was the first to break the silence between them as if they were old friends.

"Yesterday," he began, "I was bluffing. Truly, I would not have butchered you. I'd have found another way into the village."

"Oh, well, that's good of you," Runa said sarcastically, not sure if that was supposed to be reassuring or not.

"I meant you no harm is all I am trying to say. Only the old man will feel my blade unless it is to defend myself." He paused for a few minutes then went on. "Your family doesn't seem to hold much affection for you. Flynn Bloodhead explained some things to me. It sounds like you've had a difficult time of it." He was not sure if she knew that Flynn was her blood father, so he tried not to reveal more than necessary.

"Yes, I know Gorm did not father me. I am a solstice child. Usually, they are loved as a gift from Freya, but with me, it is different. Flynn is my father's biggest rival and so Gorm hates me, but it makes him feel as if he has the upper hand by keeping something of Flynn's. I also believe my mother secretly loves Flynn in her heart. She would not truly harm me because of it. I've seen her looking at Flynn in an entirely different way than she looks at Gorm."

"Yes, then why does she stay with Gorm?"

"When I was young, I overheard my mother speaking to one of the other women. One solstice, before she was married, she put seven flowers under her pillow so that she would dream of her future husband. She did and her dream prophecy was that she would marry the Jarl of our village and that man was Gorm. The gods do not take kindly when you go against their prophecies and so she went with Gorm, though it was Flynn she truly wanted. Now, as she dreamed, she is the chieftain's wife. But, every solstice festival, I watch, and she sneaks away into the forest with Flynn."

"Flynn said as much to me as well. He said she bewitched him. If I were Gorm, I would not allow my wife to lay with another man."

"Signe is beautiful and so Flynn goes willingly, but I have seen Gorm and Flynn's wife Aileen, go into the forest on Freya's night as well. With them, there is no love between husband and wife, only longing for what they cannot have. So, they all hide secret desires and there is a kind of balance in it all."

"I thought only maidens went into the forest on Freya's night?" Brand turned toward Runa and searched her face and her blue eyes.

Reaching out he plucked a leaf from her red hair, and he watched as her lightly freckled cheeks reddened. The quickening of his pulse and the rush of his blood through his veins made him want to lean in and kiss her full lips. She did not answer him, she only stilled, looking intently at him. Her cheeks flushed pink.

"Who did you dream of when you put flowers under your pillow?" His voice was soft and low when he asked, and Runa felt the heat of his body next to hers. His freshly washed scent enticed her.

"Before, I never placed the seven flowers under my pillow to dream of my future husband. I was not allowed to participate in Freya's night. My mother says I am so ugly no one would want me. Though, once, a few years ago, a young man asked after me, but Gorm declared he would never let me marry. He said I was not eligible. I am not yet twenty, so have no legal rights. Anyway, Gorm declared I should be a crone, an unmarried woman. My mother wants me to be a healer and some use to Lyngmarker. None of the men in the village will defy the Jarl and since he treats me as a thrall, everyone else does as well. The other thralls hate me because I am the Jarl's daughter, and they think I receive special treatment."

Runa shrugged and bowed her head over her bent knees as if ashamed, but then took a deep breath and looked straight into Brand's face with a defiant gleam in her eyes.

"This year, I have decided to defy them all. I will put flowers under my pillow to dream of my future husband and I'll dance with the other maidens on Freya's night. I will see if a man leaps the bonfire for me and I'll go into the woods and hope the man of my dreams follows."

There was almost an invitation in her last words and Brand stared at her. His plans did not involve young maidens or leaping over bonfires but for this beautiful girl? The possibility stared at him in the face from haunting blue eyes.

Chapter Seven

Following a great impulse, Brand reached out and caressed Runa's breast awkwardly. Runa was startled and slapped his hand and leaned away.

"What are you doing!" Runa snapped.

Brand looked slightly embarrassed, though his eyes gleamed with mischief and curiosity.

"Touching you."

"Why?" Runa's eyes opened wide, and she shivered but wasn't sure if it was because she was afraid of him or not.

The thought occurred to her, no one ever touched her unless it was to hurt her. Just for a moment, she wondered what it would be like to be touched in a gentle, affectionate way. Brand's touch had sent a thrill of excitement through her.

"You're pretty and I wanted to see what your breasts felt like. I'll not apologize for wanting to touch you." He shrugged as if it did not make a difference to him.

Runa hesitated for a long moment, not sure of what to do. He was staring down at her breasts, though what he thought he could see or feel through the dress she wore, Runa was unsure. Watching him stare at her and the way he licked his lips when he did, warmed her and made her heart flutter like a startled bird. This was something she had not considered. After a long silence between them, she gave into curiosity.

"Do you want to do it again?" She asked slowly, curious as to what he would say.

"Yes, very much so." He answered without any hesitation, his voice going hard. "But I'll not take what isn't given freely." That decisiveness settled it for her.

Runa loosened the ties and reached for the collar of her underdress and pulled it aside revealing more of her skin. Brand moved closer, reached forward, and slipped his hand within, staring at what she was revealing. It was awkward at first, but his fingers smoothed over her bare skin. His hand was cool but warmed quickly on her flesh. Her nipple tightened and stood as he moved his fingers against it and cupped her, kneading gently. Her eyes fluttered while he drew heat from her, she pressed into his hand as warmth spread throughout her body. Her lips parted and she inhaled sharply when his other hand slid up her neck and he pulled her toward him. His mouth descended on hers and his moist lips rubbed and pulled at hers in Runa's first-ever kiss.

It was strange to press her lips against a stranger's mouth. He tasted heady like mead. His lips were firm and soft at the same time, and her body felt strange. Dizzy, lethargic heat began to overwhelm her limbs and spread through her stomach. She didn't care. Runa had never been treated with such tenderness. She felt boneless as his bare chest pressed against hers. Kissing her in long caressing sweeps he tantalized her. Her hands reached around him, and she tried not to appear awkward as he lowered her back toward the blanket they sat on. His kisses became more heated. Looming over her, he pressed his hand to her breast once again.

Runa panted as his tongue touched hers and swept deeply into her mouth. He seemed to be growing more insistent and held her tight, which was a feeling she loved instantly. Other feelings he was causing in her body were new and wonderful, and she wished he would never stop. When his mouth left hers and traveled down her neck in soft bites and kisses, she held her breath as his hand pulled her tunic further aside, and then his mouth was on her breast. Her eyes flew open staring up into the blue sky through the trees sheltering them. She quivered under his caresses as he sucked gently at the sensitive flesh of her taught nipple.

A small moan escaped Runa as shocks of pleasure spread through her. Her breathing came in short pants. She bit her lower lip to stop the noises she was making, but that did not stop him from continuing. Her fingers laced through his hair and guided him to each breast so that he could give his attention to both. She lost track of the day and the hour and forgot what she was supposed to be doing, and just lived in this sweet moment, enjoying being wanted. When his hand smoothed up her skirt and found her bare leg it brought her back to herself and she squirmed, not sure if she was trying to get away or get closer. Brand's mouth found hers again then his hand found the place on her body no other person had ever touched. She was already warm and moist from his other attentions and when he found her bare core with his fingers, a growl rose from deep in his chest, and his tongue plunged even more passionately in unison with hers. The kisses, the touches on her breasts, his mouth, and his hard body pressing against hers was so wonderful she did not want to stop.

Runa knew the love act that happened between men and women. At night in the dark longhouse, she peeked through the hangings and saw men and women writhing together in different love positions. So, Runa knew what Brand was working toward. This might be her only opportunity to ever be with him in the same way as she had seen other lovers, but she did not want to jeopardize his attention by asking for too much. So, she allowed him to lead the way. Since he came into her life, he had been angry, violent, and threatening to her, her village, and her family. He wanted to kill the old man she had come to admire in such a short time. Now, he was gently insistent with affection that was meant only between lovers. Runa held her breath fascinated that this warrior seemed to want her.

Rising, he moved over her. His heated gaze held hers as if waiting for her to reject him, but she did not, just pulled him into another kiss. The hard, warmth of his manhood was so close, only the thin cloth separated them. Reveling in the affection he offered, she waited for him to go further when a voice shouted from out of the forest behind them. His mouth left hers and his head snapped up, his body stilled. Runa's eyes flew open as she recognized the voice of her brother, Vonn. He must have come looking for her.

Vonn was the most irritating of her brothers and was closest to her in age. He was the shortest of his brothers and they continuously teased him about his smaller stature. It bothered him to the point that he became very angry and mean and dissatisfied with everything in his life. Usually, Runa was the recipient of his aggression because he liked to pick on those smaller than him.

"Runa! Where are you?" Vonn's voice sounded as if it was getting closer.

Runa struggled to get out from under Brand and he pushed back onto his knees and watched her scramble backward while tugging up the front of her tunic and pushing down her underdress. Embarrassment turned her violent red. Shock and guilt made her face burn. Everything happened at once. Vonn's voice came even closer, and his shouts grew angrier. Runa turned in

Vonn's direction and called out, hoping to stop him from coming any closer.

"I'm coming!" Runa flinched at the sound of her voice, breathless and guilt-ridden. "I'm coming!"

Vonn crashed through the brush and Runa smothered a squeal. Her blood turned icy cold realizing she would be found with Brand with her skirts hiked up and her bare breasts exposed. When she turned to look where he had been kneeling between her legs, Runa found she was alone. There was no trace left of him. She was not sure what surprised her more, Vonn's appearance or Brand's disappearance.

"Runa! What in the name of all the gods are you doing? You lazy, worthless, thrall!" Angry, Vonn looked around suspiciously.

Thinking quickly, Runa's eyes darted around, and she spotted the basket of bathing implements, the cloth for drying, and soap remembering her mother had ordered her to bathe.

"I was just washing! Mother ordered me to!" Pulling her legs underneath her, Runa clutched the drying cloth to her chest and blushed. She had to hide the relief she felt that Brand managed to slip away quietly. It did indeed look as if Runa was alone seeing to her personal needs.

"Well get your lazy arse back to the house. Mother is looking for you and you will pay for it if you keep her waiting."

Vonn either had not noticed her flushed state or he did not care. Like all his other family members he was never kind to her, and this time was no different. His eyes swept her wrinkled clothes and damp, messy hair with a contemptuous scowl. He did not waste any more time on her, he just turned and left.

Runa crumbled with relief, threw everything in her basket and bundled the towel up, pulled on her slippers, stood, and brushed the wrinkles from her dress. Her hand smoothed her hair back plucking leaves from the long, damp tresses. Her body still pulsed with desire, her heart fluttered with uncertainty and her eyes searched the edges of the river, looking for Brand. He was gone. She stopped for a moment and closed her eyes, recalling his kisses. Her fingers reached up and traced her bottom lip where his mouth had slid against hers so passionately. When she opened her eyes again, she slowly looked out. Across the river, Brand stood at the forest edge watching her. Their eyes held and an understanding passed between them. Or maybe it was her imagination? Embarrassed, Runa bent, gathered her things, and whirled away, heading back to the lodge where her mother waited for her.

Chapter Eight

After leaving Runa, Brand returned to Flynn Bloodhead's house. He felt slightly guilty that he left her alone to be found by her brother. However, it was best if he was not caught slaking his lust by trying to take advantage of her. What was going through his mind when he kissed her and proceeded to go further with her, he was not completely sure. He had acted on instinct and was only thinking of her softness, enticing beauty, and sweetness, at the time. There was a shortage of those things in his life and Runa had almost instantly become the embodiment of those things to him. That she was innocent, and he had almost taken that innocence was now a bit alarming. He decided it would be best if he stayed away from Runa.

For the rest of the day, Brand drank mead with Flynn Bloodhead, while everyone in the village ran back and forth preparing for the first night of the solstice festival. Men were out hunting and gathering and chopping wood to fuel the bonfires that would burn throughout the entire twelve-day celebration. He scowled, not very pleased with himself every time he thought of the early morning. Runa's lure had been difficult to resist, and he kissed her and caressed her without thinking of the consequences. The truth was, as soon as he killed the old man, he would go and leave this place, *and her*, behind.

It was this day! The solstice, the longest day of the year, and the goddess's magic in the air were making him crazy. He had been to similar celebrations when he was young and knew what had transpired during the centuries that the festival was held. As he traveled, searching out the men who betrayed and slaughtered his family, he did not have time or opportunity to participate in many such traditions. Now, he must wait until the twelve days of revelry were over and he could slay the last enemy and move on. Breaking the rules of celebration during a time of love and fertility made him fearful of the gods' displeasure and retribution. He needed Odin's blessing to finish his quest.

Thinking about what would happen after he killed the last enemy had not occurred to him, yet here he was. Looking down into his drinking horn, Brand narrowed his eyes remembering. Eiland Biersson was one of the men he had admired most during those fateful days when his crew came to Brand's family farm. Shame flooded him when he thought about how he once wanted to be like him. He had been a young boy, dreaming of becoming a great warrior and going Viking on the great ocean and down the wide rivers seeking his fortune. Eiland had ruffled his hair, taken an interest in him, practiced wooden swords with Brand, and told him he would be a great warrior someday. Now, the thought that he, even once, had soft feelings for those men made him want to retch violently. Eiland Biersson was the worst because he had considered him a close friend and teacher, and that is one reason Brand had saved him for last.

#

The hour came for the gathering. Songs, games, banquets, and sacrifices for the gods and to the ancestor spirits, would occur over the next twelve days straight. The celebration would be accompanied by feasting and drinking on an almost gluttonous level. People gathered as the sun approached the surrounding mountains to the west, this was the day when it ruled longer than usual. The evening air was warm and fresh. Smoke from cookfires drifted and carried the smell of roasting meat on the breeze. A festive mood permeated the forest as everyone made their way to the central clearing where the bonfire was yet to be lit. Brand lingered behind, not wanting to intrude on a celebration that had nothing to do with him with people he did not know. Flynn Bloodhead threw an arm around his shoulder and pulled him along with a good-natured laugh.

Gorm gave a long-winded welcome speech to start the solstice festival. Signe, dressed in her finest ceremonial gown, carried a torch from their home hearth and lit the main bonfire. Costly brooches on each shoulder gleamed with silver and amber jewels. A long chain hung down to her waist with the keys to the Jarl's great hall. There were many prayers and much singing, and the ceremony officially began.

Brand looked through the crowd for the old man, but his enemy must have been too sick to participate in the festivities because he was not present. He gave some thought to sneaking away and finishing the old man in his bed, but that would not be honorable or satisfying. It would all be over in twelve days. He had been patient for ten long years and an end to his hunting was in sight, but his desire to kill the old man outweighed everything else.

Beside him, Flynn Bloodhead was staring across the fire to where Signe sat, eyes smoldering with lust. She was doing her best not to stare back at him but failed. Brand saw the heated looks passing between them and knew that they would sneak away that night and meet each other in the forest as they did every year. That thought had Brand looking for Runa.

When the feast was ready people flocked to the food, and the mead flowed. Runa kept distant from her mother and ignored Gorm's glares. She acted as she always did, like a thrall, working and not part of the celebration. Her older brother Vidar was busy flirting with one of the maidens he had his eye on, Bjorn was stuffing his face with venison, and Vonn was swaying already too deep in his drinking horn to be of any use to anyone. Runa could not eat, she was too nervous, but she forced down some smoked boar the village cooks roasted as this was Freya's sacrificial animal and she wanted the goddess's blessing tonight. She also stole a honey cake as it was such a rare occasion that she was allowed to eat one of the sweets. Her plan was set to defy her parents and so Runa carried pitchers brimming with mead to the men around the gathering and enjoyed the feast as if she did not have a care in the world. No one noticed when she slipped away.

It was the time for all the maidens to gather around a tall pole hung with colorful ribbons and set firmly in the ground. Dressed lavishly in white with slit skirts and wide corded belts weaved with spirals and runes, they lined up. Silver and amber beads were hung around their slender necks indicating their wealth and adding to their appeal. Weaved flower crowns were set atop their long, golden, brown, or red flowing hair. Their long legs flashed seductively bare as they moved into place. They all looked like goddesses in the early evening light, giggling while gathered around the pole and waiting for the dance to begin. When the drums and flutes and instruments started, each maiden took her place and grabbed a ribbon tied to the pole. Soon, their voices rose in song and their bare feet began to pound the grassy ground. Runa was not among them.

As soon as the circle began to move, another maiden with flaming red hair crowned with lavender flowers darted out from the forest to take her place. Though late, Runa had finally come.

Casting a glance toward Gorm and Signe, Brand saw neither had yet noticed Runa joined the dancing maidens. Both frowned when the dancing was well underway, and they finally spotted Runa among the dancers.

Fury reddened Gorm's face, and he ground his teeth, but he could do nothing about it now. It would be embarrassing for him to deny Runa her place with the other maidens, as she was of age, and she was his acknowledged daughter. Pulling her away now would interrupt the feast. He could not risk bringing discord and bad luck to a night that was supposed to be full of laughter and good cheer. Scowling, he looked away lamenting that this is what happened when he claimed a daughter not of his blood.

Brand did not imagine the promising glare of retribution Gorm gave to Runa. She did not seem to care but glowed with an inner happiness and joy that was almost infectious as the dancing and singing continued.

All the maidens danced around the pole weaving in and out, flowing back and forth in the traditional dance. Their white legs flashed, and their bare feet stepped sure upon the grassy ground. They were graceful and enticing as they performed the moves. Runa's white smile beamed with every step. Her long, loose hair swayed as she danced like a flickering flame and, in the spirit of the dance, the maidens welcomed her in. The presence of the goddess filled her, and Runa understood as she joined them that this was a night when magic would fill her, a solstice child, and grant her greatest desires.

As she danced, she purposely did not look at Gorm or her mother, but instead, let her eyes search the crowd as she circled the pole, dancing the steps in time with the others. Earlier that morning, the thought crossed her mind that the answer to all of her dreams was Brand Keitelsson. What they started in the forest that morning, she intended to finish later that night. All she had to do was catch his attention and inflame his interest with her dancing. No one could stop her now.

On the final circle around the pole, Runa was breathless from laughing and singing. Her eyes sparkled, and she found who she wanted. Brand was standing a little bit outside the circle of people who were clapping and singing, drinking, and watching the maidens dance. The rhythmic pounding of the drum kept the beat. Young men jostled for position forming a circle around the clearing in front of the bonfire trying to catch the eye of their chosen maiden as the dancing continued. Runa looked at no one from her village, but directly toward Brand. They were two outsiders who could offer each other something neither of them had expected to find. As she danced, she kept her gaze firmly locked on his. The magic of Freya's night enclosed them both.

Darkness had crept upon the celebration and the dancing would go on through the night, but the full moon was overhead signaling midnight, and the bonfire crackled with white-hot coals. It was time. The drums beat and men gathered and fought to be the first ones to leap over the bonfire for good luck and to chase a willing maiden into the forest. Now was the time of the celebration where the goddess of fertility ruled, the men were filled with lust and the young women were filled with hope.

As the dance ended, Runa moved to hide on the edges of the gathering but kept watching for the one she chose. It irked her to hide from Gorm but felt it wisest to do so. She had been too nervous to approach Brand all evening but hoped that he would leap over the bonfire for her and give chase. Her stomach flipped thinking about the caresses and kisses they shared earlier that morning. She hoped it was an indication of things to come. If he desired her, then all her prayers to the goddess would be answered, her wishes fulfilled. Closing her eyes, she cast her desire out into the night and imagined bewitching Brand and drawing him to her, as Mother did to Flynn Bloodhead.

Signe also waited until the celebration was in full force and when Gorm was occupied by his drinking, she stared boldly at Flynn Bloodhead. Confident in her beauty, sending her witchery across the bonfire to him, she called to him. The moment he rose to his feet catching her eye, Signe slipped away. Flynn silently backed into the shadows and followed.

Runa switched her gaze to watch Gorm. He was very drunk and did not notice his wife slip away to meet with his greatest enemy. Aileen, Flynn's wife, was a few feet away and he sobered quickly upon seeing her lingering by the fire trying to catch his eye. Forgetting his wife, his enemies, and his duties, Gorm announced he was going to piss in the bushes and lumbered away. No one noticed Aileen suddenly went missing too, except Runa. Now was her opportunity. She moved into the light of the fire and sent her magic toward Brand.

Over the burning logs, warriors were leaping, and with feigned cries of distress and high-pitched giggles, maidens fled wishing to be chased. The fire crackled and spat, and the smoke carried her spell. Runa waited for Brand to see her. He seemed to be searching for someone and doubt flooded her. Her hope was he was looking for her. His eyes finally found her face, Runa's smile swelled with allure, wanting him to see her.

The drums and music continued the pagan beat while singing and shouting filled the air. The bonfire light glowed upon Runa's bright red hair as it flowed caught by the soft wind. The magic of the solstice night sparkled in her eyes. Her brilliant white dress made her skin luminous like the full moon above. She looked like a goddess stepping out of an enchanted forest who beckoned Brand with a mysterious call. The blood rushed through his veins and heated his muscles, forcing him to move his feet. In the branches above where Runa stood, a raven stirred, and Brand felt the ominous presence of the gods pushing him forward. Magic and mystery summoned and promised pleasure.

No one noticed the hopeful smile Runa gave Brand and that was enough encouragement for him. He took two steps back, ran, and leaped over the bonfire with ease, following two other men who went after other maidens. His boots struck the ground a few feet away from the tree Runa stood by and as soon as he landed, she whirled and ran. Like a doe trying to outrun a hunter, she was fleet of foot and ran sure. No one noticed whom the stranger chased into the darkness of the forest. The drumbeat pounded the night air swirling in the undeniable magic of Freya's night.

Chapter Nine

Runa took off running as soon as Brand's boots hit the ground. She was elated and, though she hardly knew this man, keenly sensed him giving chase. The thought that she had almost succumbed to him that morning and ruined what was now going to happen this special night, frightened her a little. It had seemed natural at the time, and she wanted to be with him but was now glad they had been interrupted.

The full moon overhead made the forest glow with a silvery light and the scent of pine gave the forest a crisp clean fragrance. Hearing the river ahead, the magic of the goddess filled Runa as she slowed and waited for her solstice lover. Pounding the forest loam behind her was the sound of Brand's boots. When she reached the small clearing she had prepared for them, she stopped and waited. A startled owl hooted as it rose in the air and the night held its breath waiting for Brand to appear.

Brand watched the magic unfolding in front of him as Runa ran. The flash of her white dress and the promise of her seductive smile had him recklessly putting on speed to catch her.

It was only a few heartbeats and then he was there in front of her. Brand did not wait, and Runa did not play coy. They flew into each other's arms, eager to continue the embrace they began earlier that morning.

Brand held Runa and crushed her lips with his. Earlier, when he had seen her smile at him across the bonfire, the primal urge to have her was more than he could withstand. Though he was a stranger to the people of this village and hardly knew this girl, resisting was impossible. Something happened to him, whether it was the magic of the solstice night, Freya's interference, or the memory of Runa's kisses and soft breasts, he could not stop to figure out what drove him. The goddess had seemed to whisper in his ear urging him to leap the flames and give chase. He obeyed. Now Runa was there with him, in his arms and she was gasping his name, and pulling his shirt up and over his head while he removed her belt and dress. Her small hands smoothed over his bare skin, and it was as if the rest of their clothes were spirited away by magic. Her breasts were pressed against him, and he threaded his fingers through her thick hair as his kisses engulfed her.

The soft scent of heather lingered on her skin. A sheen of sweat was on his brow, and she kissed his heated cheeks. When they slowly sunk to the cool forest bed, Brand knew nothing else at that moment but the softness of her skin and her sweet taste. He lowered his head to her breasts, kissing their fullness. The sound of her quickening breathing spurred Brand on. When her hands tugged at him and her legs opened, he returned to the place he had thought about since that morning. Now, there would be no interruptions to stop him. She gasped as he eased his way in. He felt her hands move down his bare back and settle on his behind. She pressed and he surged deep. He breathed a sigh of relief as her warmth embraced his scalding flesh. She whimpered as he penetrated her maidenhead and then moaned in pleasure as he began to move.

Brand embraced beautiful Runa, sinking deep inside her then withdrawing only to sink in deep again. The fragrance of flowers drifted from her hair and her lips tasted honey-sweet. Slowly, his hips moved, and he growled, savoring the feelings coursing through his body. He was tight with need and his heart raced with his blood. Then he rolled and pulled her on top of him and the moon overhead shone down on her raised above him. The magic of Freya's night descended like glittering dew speckling her skin with stars. He could see Runa's beautiful face illuminated from above. Her lips were parted slightly as if surprised by what their bodies were doing. Brand stared into her eyes, and she stared back at him. He moved, thrusting upward watching the effect his body had on hers. They held each other's gaze as the pleasure mounted and they undulated together. Brand felt the moment pleasure found her as the pulsing clenching his hardness within her soft body. Pulling her down, his mouth sought hers and he kissed her hard as she climaxed, and he released his seed a few thrusts later. He held his breath as he emptied into her and kissed his solstice lover in the moonlight until she was breathless. Brand pulled her down next to him and they lay together, letting the ardor of lovemaking cool. The music of the night serenaded them with the goddess's pleased voice who pulled her blessing around them.

Runa's red hair looked dark in the night and her body was whitened by the light of the solstice moon. When the magic of the night took over them again a short time later, it seemed as if the goddess herself looked down at them pleased as they joined once again.

There was a lot of heavy breathing and gasps of pleasure, touching, and a small bit of joyous cursing on Brand's side. His words expressed his astonishment at being right where he was. The scent of their bodies sweating together in the warm night lingered between them. The rustle of the wind in the leaves marked the goddess passing and drowned out the sound of singing. Distant drums beat the rhythm their bodies followed. When their lust for each other was quenched, they lay entwined. Before falling asleep Runa marveled at what happened between her and Brand. Never had she been treated with such tenderness, such kindness, and passion. The soft way he touched her and the feelings his body caused in hers was overwhelming.

"More," was her last thought, *"Goddess! I want more of this!"* and she fell into a peaceful sleep.

Morning came and Runa woke beside Brand, who slept peacefully. The look on his face was calm and his brow was tan, smooth, and absent of his usual frown. Runa looked at him for a moment then carefully tried to rise. Mother would be looking for her soon and there was food to prepare for the morning meal and endless chores to be done to prepare for the second day of the festival. She sat up and Brand reached for her, pulling her down. He moved to cover her with his body.

"Warriors sleep very lightly, Runa. Where do you think you're escaping to?"

Brand began kissing her neck. Runa's eyes grew large as she felt his firm body pressing against her. She understood what he intended.

"I have to go. My mother will be looking for me. If she finds out about this, I'll be trouble."

"No," Brand pushed her arms above her head and held both wrists with one hand so she couldn't escape. She understood his playfulness and smiled when his head bent, and he kissed her neck while she struggled half-heartedly in his grip. Soon their ardor was quenched, and they lay gasping.

"Please let me up Brand. I've got to be back before my mother awakens. We've many more days of the festival to be together."

Brand released her and rolled away then watched as Runa reached for her dress and the ceremonial belt that she had worn the night before. She was smiling widely at him, and he leaned up on one elbow and plucked a leaf from her hair.

"Say you'll meet me again tonight, Runa?" Brand asked.

"Yes, I will if I can get away. Now, I have to go." She quickly bent to kiss him on the lips and then leaped up and darted away. Brand grabbed his britches and looked for his boots. A rare smile crossed his lips and he felt strangely...content.

\#

Gorm had an aching head and a sour taste in his mouth. He had awoken alone in the forest, with his britches bunched around his ankles and his bare behind was cold. His lust had been satisfied by Aileen, he recalled, and so he was not bothered by the state he found himself in. Glad there was no one around to see his embarrassment, a wave of satisfaction hit him as he remembered plundering Flynn Bloodhead's wife. It gave him no end of pleasure to have had his biggest rival's red-headed wife bent over and moaning Gorm's name. After that, he did not remember much else. Now, it was time to return to the longhouse and prepare for the day's duties, which involved many speeches, rituals, and much more drinking. Gorm's mouth was dry and all he could think of was a horn of mead to chase away the aftermath of last night's merriment. He relieved himself on a bush, pulled up his britches, and turned his steps toward home.

Ahead of him, he heard voices and slowed his steps. Peering through the bushes he saw two people wrapped in the throes of morning lovemaking. He watched with curiosity and realized it was the stranger who had recently come to his village. The same man who wanted to kill Eiland Biersson. As soon as he was done, the young warrior lifted off his lover and Gorm saw *Runa* get up and reach for her clothing. Gorm's eyes filled with the sight of her naked body and his mind filled with rage. She had defied his order that she not participate in this particular solstice ritual. He wanted to stomp into the clearing and beat her then and there, but something made him pause. Perhaps it was the mischievous Loki who whispered in his ear urging him to wait, telling him that there was more satisfying revenge to be had if he was patient. So, he did; Gorm waited until Runa dressed and ran off and left the stranger alone. After a few moments, he stepped into the clearing, catching the stranger by surprise.

Brand slowly raised his head and looked at Gorm stepping out of the bushes and his mind quickly realized two things. Gorm most likely saw him with Runa which could go badly for her. The second thing was he had just taken the maidenhead of Gorm's only daughter. If the excuse of Freya's night of the solstice festival was enough, then all might be well. Judging by the look on the man's face, Brand decided that it would not be enough.

"Enjoying yourself?" Gorm grumbled.

Brand reached for his other boot and casually slipped it on and tied it before standing to face Gorm.

"Enjoying watching?" Brand frowned, folding his arms across his chest.

"Runa is forbidden from taking part in any of the solstice rituals. I suppose she failed to mention that to you before you took her maidenhead."

"Your *daughter* is of age and therefore free to take part in the festivities if it is her wish. Why do you deny her this rite of passage into womanhood?"

"Because she is under my rule, and I say what she can and cannot do. She is no better than one of my thralls and I don't want her getting her belly full of a babe. I don't need another mouth to feed. You are an arrogant pup and you're sticking your cock where it doesn't belong. If a child comes from this night, I'll feed it to the wolves rather than suffer another solstice child!"

Gorm's hatred for Runa overwhelmed Brand even though he knew the reason for it. He also had not thought that a baby might come from last night's solstice joining, but he would think of that later.

"What kind of father hates his only daughter so much that he would say such things?"

"The kind that thinks she is *my daughter* and what I say about her is none of your concern. The truth is I don't care if you hump her until she can't walk. You are only here for a short time at the mercy of my generosity and hospitality which you have breached by sleeping with Runa. I won't break the peace of the solstice celebration and anger the gods, but come the day when it is over, there will be nothing stopping me from doing as I please with you and with my *daughter*."

Brand hated the scornful way Gorm said, *'daughter'* as if Runa were something to be ashamed of. He did not understand it and felt a surge of protection toward his solstice lover. The truth was that he had not thought past the pleasure of the ritual. He had been caught up in the goddess's magic and the festive mood of the celebration. He would leave once his enemy was delivered into his hands and his thirst for vengeance was quenched. He had no intention of taking anyone with him.

"You've given your word there is to be a battle between me and my enemy. All you have to do is remember that agreement, or I will have your head as well as his, cut by my blade!" The thought that Gorm might be hinting he might go back on their deal infuriated him.

Gorm was a little surprised at the young man's threat. Brand looked strong and fast, but he was young and Gorm was broader and more experienced. The blade at the stranger's side was of good Norse steel, and he had enough swagger to possibly make good on his boasts.

"Stay away from Runa or you'll be meeting my blade at the end of the solstice festival, not the old man's."

He issued this threat with a snarl while leaning close to Brand's face, the foul scent of stale mead on his breath. He snarled once more, before stomping away, making sure to bump into Brand's shoulder as he passed.

Gorm left the boy to piss in his pants fearing his retribution, for now, he was going to go and deal with Runa.

Chapter Ten

By the time Gorm returned to the longhouse he had a plan worked out in his mind. The women were just getting food and mead laid out for the early meal. The warmth of the morning air warmed the hall. He snatched a horn and downed the cool liquid, relieving his aching head just a bit. Many of his warriors were strewn about the hall sleeping off the night's drink. One or two sat at the table with pounding heads propped in their hands, still half asleep. Gorm wondered if the men on watch were alert and sober and made a mental note to send Vidar or Bjorn to check on them. He scanned the great hall, looking for Runa's redhead among the women, but did not spot her. That suited his purpose, for now. He made his way past the sleeping men and women and went toward the small stall that served as Eiland Biersson's sick room.

Pulling the cloth curtain aside he went in and was pleased to find that the old man was awake. Gorm let the curtain fall requiring privacy for this conversation. Eiland stared as Gorm pulled up a stool and sat down. He slowly ladled porridge into his mouth and did not stop eating when his host entered. It was clear that his visitor had something on his mind.

"How are you feeling old man?" Gorm asked, not truly interested, but he wanted to start the conversation on a good footing.

"I'm mending, the leg is still painful, but the sickness has left my lungs thanks to Runa's tending."

Eiland surveyed Gorm and narrowed his eyes at him. Something told him this was not just a visit to find out how well he fared.

"Tell me old man, the place you come from...do you have a wife and children waiting for you?"

"No," Eiland looked away quickly, but not before Gorm saw a flicker of sadness in his eyes. "No, the boy has hunted me and my warrior brothers for ten long years. I never found time for a wife. There is nothing left for me where I come from."

"Can you still get it up?" Gorm leaned forward and asked without a hint of reserve in his voice. "Can you bed a woman?"

"I am still strong and virile. My cock works just fine if it is any of your concern." Eiland began to wonder where this line of questioning was going. "But I don't expect to live long enough to put it to much use."

"I have a proposal for you. As soon as you're on your feet again, I will give you Runa as a wife. You deserve to have a life after running from that fiend who has been pursuing you for so long. Just take the girl away from here. I can't stand the sight of her anymore. She defies my orders, breaks my rules, and challenges my patience. I am sick of looking at her ugly face."

"You are wrong, Runa is a young, beautiful, *desirable* woman. She would be wasted on an old man like me. Besides, I've nothing to pay a bride-price. Why do you hate the girl so much you'd marry her off to a man you hardly know?"

"It is none of your concern." Gorm would not look him in the eye. "The bride-price is to take her away. Just kill the boy is all you have to do."

"If you want my cooperation, I must know the truth about this girl." Eiland's face turned hard.

"She is from the seed of my enemy and not my blood child." Gorm was red in the face making the confession.

"Ah…," Eiland nodded with understanding, "yet, you call her daughter. You claimed her as your own."

"She is a solstice child and protected under the law or I'd have left her to be eaten by the wolves as an infant. I would have cut Signe's hair off, sold her as a slave, or killed her had she done this at any other time, but…" Gorm faltered and refused to reveal anything more.

"A solstice child?" Eiland's eyes grew wide, "so, she is a lucky one."

"She is an insult to me! Now, will you take her?" Impatience salted Gorm's words.

Eiland considered for a moment then shook his head slowly.

"I do not doubt that when I fight against the boy, I'll lose. I'll be too dead to wed or bed her." Eiland chuckled at his little joke thinking the whole conversation was ludicrous.

"What if I *guarantee* that you will win?" Gorm leaned close and lowered his voice.

There was a long pause between them.

"And...how could you guarantee that?" Eiland leaned back suddenly taking Gorm very seriously.

#

Runa had done it. With the goddess guiding her, she was a woman now and had enjoyed the first night of the solstice celebration to the fullest. Brand, the strange warrior from far away, had leaped over the bonfire for *her*. They had lain together with the blessing of Freya and the solstice night. Now she held onto the hope that he would be her husband and take her away from this place. Her imagination ran wild thinking of adventures, seeing new lands together, of nights full of loving, and endless days of happiness. She would even convince him to teach her how to use a sword and bow, and they would fight side by side. Fantasies filled her mind and in them, she wore silver armor and stood by Brand's side, a true shield maiden. For now, she had to slip back into the longhouse, staying hidden in the shadows and avoiding getting caught by her mother or Gorm or her brothers.

As it turned out, everyone was still sleeping off the night's festivities and no one was looking for her. Thus, it stood to reason that no one knew she had spent the night with Brand, the stranger. Her heart took a little leap as she remembered their lovemaking under the moonlight. It had been more than she could have ever hoped for. Head filled with dreams she walked through the dark hallway toward her sleeping stall.

A slim figure stepped out of the shadows abruptly and stopped her. It was Ida one of the women who worked in the house as a cook.

"And just where have *you* been?"

Ida stood blocking Runa's passage and she stepped back. This seemed to be the woman's favorite past-time, sneaking up on Runa and interrogating her. Even though Runa was Gorm's daughter, she had no standing and because he treated her badly, everyone else did as well. The other servants and slaves in the house hated her because they felt she got special treatment, and her family despised her because she was Flynn Bloodhead's child.

"I, I am going to check on Eiland Biersson," Runa said quietly.

"I've already taken him his breakfast because you were out lazing around again. Where were you this time…" an idea must have struck Ida because her eyes widened, and she stepped closer to Runa. "You were out acting like a Hóra on Freya's night! Why you worthless little thrall. Just wait until Gorm hears about this."

"I wasn't doing anything, Ida. I was just out using the privy. I overslept, that's all. Please don't tell Gorm any lies about me." Runa could not help but beg a little. She thought of bribing the horrible woman with her bone comb but realized it would confirm where Runa had been and that she lied.

"Hmph," Ida snorted. She reached out and pulled Runa's hair like she always did. As soon as her red locks were free of Ida's claw-like grasp, she fled.

Slipping into her small sleeping stall, she changed quickly, combed the leaves and tangles from her hair, washed her face and body with cold water, and put on a clean tunic. Holding her head high, she left and went to begin her chores. Her mind wanted to forget Ida and her threats and instead wandered back over the night's events. Her body warmed with the thought of the dancing, the thrill of Brand leaping over the bonfire for her, the chase, and what came afterward. It felt as if the goddess had truly blessed her last night and she felt assured that her luck was changing.

Right now, all she wanted to do was to lie in the sunshine and relive what she and Brand had done, but she had duties to attend to. One such duty was to check on Grandfather or rather, Eiland Biersson. She admonished herself not to think of him as her grandfather as he truly was no blood relation to her at all. If Brand killed Eiland, well, she did not want to think about that. Having found him wounded and tended to him in his sick bed she felt responsible for him, and a little bit attached if she were to admit it. He was kind to her, told her stories, and made her imagination leap with possibilities beyond the drudgery of her life.

Blood debts were part of the Norse life and Runa, having been treated like a thrall since she was a young child, had no part in them. She couldn't think of a way to stop Brand's revenge and had to accept that he had to do what he thought was best.

Grabbing what she needed, Runa strode to the back of the hall where Eiland's stall was. She ducked out of sight when she saw Gorm heading to the same place she was going. Stopping just outside the curtained doorway, she listened to Gorm's conversation with Eiland while waiting for him to leave. She did not want to go in and face Gorm's censure and was going to leave but then heard *her* name mentioned.

Her heart pounded with fear as she leaned closer and heard Gorm offer her to Eiland as a wife and he accepted her with a laugh. Gorm's hatred for Runa filled the conversation and she felt frozen, horrified, and embarrassed at the same time. How could this be when Eiland was supposed to battle Brand, and he might not live through the day after the solstice celebration? Her head began to buzz, but she made herself focus and listen as Gorm went on to explain. Her blood froze at his next words.

"What if I *guarantee* that you'd win?" Gorm's voice asked.

"And...how could you guarantee that?" Eiland's voice rose in interest.

"Today is the wrestling match. My son Vidar is my best fighter and will be participating in the competition. He is as strong as a grizzly bear and as mean as a rabid wolf. I'll make sure he injures the pup just enough so that he is compromised when you fight him. Signe can slip some herbs into his wine that will loosen his bowels, turn his blood to water, and weaken him. If you've any skill with your sword at all, you'll kill him and when you do, I'll give you Runa."

"I'll have to think about this for a while. It seems a dishonorable way to win a fight." Eiland seemed hesitant.

"Is it dishonorable to want to live? To want to have a comely young wife warming your bed for the rest of your days? Runa will give you strong sons. Besides, I think what the boy has done is dishonorable. Hunting you and your men, killing you all one by one, denying you life's simple pleasures, it goes against our way of life as Norsemen."

Gorm's voice turned to ice and his next words were spat out with such venom that Runa shivered.

"She is the daughter of my enemy abiding under my roof. Her very presence is an insult to me. I am tired of her and want her dead or gone, but she is a solstice child and has some protection under the law. Why must I repeat myself? I will give you a bag of gold and two silver arm rings, a horse, and supplies if you take this burden off my hands. All you have to do is kill the boy."

Runa had heard enough. Carefully, she backed away from the doorway, turned, and fled. Brand needed to know what Gorm had planned for him.

Chapter Eleven

Brand sat beside a fire with Flynn Bloodhead and some of his warriors. They ate porridge sweetened with honey and dried fruit, and munched on freshly baked bread and cold boar, to break their fast. Though Brand had not drunk as much mead or ale as the others the night before and did not have an aching head, he had a head full of difficult thoughts. As the others laughed, traded stories, challenges, friendly insults, and bragged about their wrestling skills, he thought of Runa.

Runa was something he had never expected to find. She was beautiful, kind, and a good, hard-working woman. She had been a virgin last night but displayed an intuitive skill while lovemaking and had pleasured him fully. Even now the thought of her made his body stir. Reprimanding his thoughts, and his overactive cock, he reminded himself of his purpose for being there. Eiland Biersson had to die at the strike of Brand's sword. His family must be avenged so that their spirits could rest easily. He was determined that no distracting female would stop him from doing just that. As he sometimes did, he relived that fateful night in his mind. Once again, he heard his mother's cries in his memories and felt the hot flames of his home burning his face. He saw once again, in his memory, his father and brothers ruthlessly cut down. Now, with his enemy in reach, he was being forced to wait to take his final revenge. The end of the solstice festival could not come soon enough.

As his mind focused on the present, eyes rising from staring into the hot red flames of the fire, Brand saw another red. It was Runa's long russet braid falling over her shoulder. She was standing in the trees beckoning to him, trying to gain his attention. Her face was pale, and he could tell she was in a hurry to speak to him. His body stirred and his desires flared when he saw her, and he rose to leave. No one paid much attention to him as he casually walked away.

Over the rim of his drinking horn, Flynn watched Brand the stranger follow Runa into the forest. He watched as they rushed away together. A trickle of satisfaction flowed through his veins and Flynn grinned.

Once inside the trees, Brand went toward Runa. His heart was pounding, and his blood rushed with the thought of embracing her once again. She was leading him away, deeper into the forest and the privacy of the thick trees would allow them to be alone together. Though he knew he should not follow, she was too big a lure for his senses.

Then she finally turned and rushed into his arms. They kissed as if they had been days apart instead of only an hour or two. Alarm flashed in Brand's mind as he realized he was becoming too attached to this red-haired beauty with sad blue eyes. As he struggled to pull her skirts up and caress her bare thigh, Runa pulled away.

"Brand, wait, you must listen to me," she gasped and pulled out of his arms.

Brand let her go. She was out of breath from kissing, but he wanted her out of breath from lovemaking.

"What is it?" He said a bit more impatiently than he intended.

"I overheard Gorm speaking to Grandfather."

"Grandfather?" Brand didn't know why this mattered. "Who is your grandfather?"

"No, I mean Eiland Biersson, he is…well, he is not truly my grandfather but as I have been tending his wounds and sickness, he asked me to call him that."

"You're very friendly with my enemy," Brand growled, flooded with irritation, he turned and stomped off.

Runa followed him. Running ahead of him, she stopped in front of him and placed her palms on his chest to stop him from leaving before hearing her out. She looked up at him with alarm all over her face.

"Please, you must forget that for now and listen to me. Gorm is going to make sure you are injured and sick when you fight so that Eiland Biersson can kill you. Then Gorm is going to give *me* to Eiland for his *wife!* Once you are dead and I am his, Eiland is going to take me away, that is the bargain they have struck."

"How? How is all this going to take place?" Brand stopped to listen though his vision began to swim red. The berserker inside him tilted his head back to howl.

"I overheard Gorm say that today, at the wrestling, Vidar will challenge you. He is going to injure you badly enough to assure your defeat. Gorm is also going to have my mother, put a weakening herb in your drink so that Vidar will overpower you. It will make you sick so that when you fight Eiland he will kill you and I'll have to marry an old man! Gorm will be rid of me and…you'll be dead."

Missing the sadness in Runa's voice as she finished her warning, Brand stopped to clear his mind of bloodlust and tried to think clearly. So, his enemy conspired to cheat destiny and a new enemy stood in the way of his revenge. When victory, vengeance, and retribution were at hand, Brand was to be wounded and poisoned to die a dishonorable death at the hands of a coward.

"I have cheated death and prevailed against my enemies many times. I am not afraid of Gorm, Vidar, or the man you call, grandfather." Brand was enraged that Runa was so intimate with his enemy. "It is a shame you are so close to the man because I am going to grind his bones into the earth, and no one will remember his name, only his foul deeds! If Gorm or Vidar get in my way, I'll kill them too!"

When she didn't speak to deny the accusation, Brand pushed past Runa and left her watching him go. The thought that Runa might love his enemy was fueling the angry fire burning in his head.

"Wait!" she finally did run after him. "What are you going to do? If you get hurt and are killed, it would...*I* would be..." She ran out of words, but her eyes were blazing with fear.

Brand stared at her trying to see behind her fear and judge what was within her mind and heart. The slight breeze blew her beautiful hair back and her cheeks blushed, pleading with her blue eyes that only hours before had burned with passion. His thoughts flashed back remembering the swell of her breasts sprinkled lightly with freckles and the softness of her body under his. The taste of her lips, the smell of her woman's passion called him, but the warrior he was did not trust the lure of her who called his enemy such an honorable endearment as *"grandfather."* The desperation in her sweet voice called him out of his rage.

"Take me away Brand. Let us leave this place together, *tonight*. Don't wrestle Vidar, there is no shame in not participating. Take nothing to eat or drink from my mother. I'll pack some provisions and meet you in the glade where we made love last night under the solstice moon. Let us become husband and wife, and together we can go out into the world and conquer anything life throws in our path. Take me away from here Brand. *Please!*"

It suddenly dawned on his suspicious mind what she was doing, and Brand grabbed her by the arms and pushed her back. Shoving her hard against a tree, she winced. He lowered his face toward her, and his eyes turned icy as he gritted his teeth trying to remember that it was wrong to hit a woman.

"You would have me run away like a coward when my final revenge is at hand? Do you love Eiland Biersson so much that you would ask me not to kill him? Let me warn you the man has no honor and is a coward. He was the last man who stood by and watched my mother be defiled, my father and brothers killed, and my home burned to the ground. Whatever they think they can do to me they are wrong. I do not need a wife and I have no wish to tie myself to the people who harbored my enemy and conspired against me. I will kill that old man who betrayed me, and I will leave this place and *you* behind!"

Brand let go of Runa as the color drained from her face and then it flared bright red with embarrassment. Tears filled her eyes and ran down her cheeks as she turned and fled. Brand watched her go while trying hard to tamp down the rage he felt. In the next moment, he regretted his harsh words but realized they were necessary and still true. Nothing had changed. The end of the solstice festival and the battle against his final foe could not come soon enough for him. When this place was nothing, but a memory and the last enemy's head hung from his belt he would leave it and *everyone* else behind.

Chapter Twelve

The rules of wrestling were fairly simple. Two opponents faced each other and the one who was thrown to the ground first lost. If a wrestler pushed the other to his knees, then the winner could also be declared the victor. If both fell to the ground at the same time, they wrestled to keep each other down and the one who got to his feet first would be declared the winner. To extend the fun, the best two out of three rounds between opponents would win. Punching, kicking, eye gouging, biting, or cheating of any kind was frowned upon. Opponents were chosen by lots or by individual challenge.

The younger men began the competition early in the day and worked their way up in the ranks until they lost. When there were no more takers the winner would be declared among the youths. Next, the older, more experienced warriors wrestled, and the bouts went on until a champion in that rank was declared.

Everyone gathered in the wide clearing where a circle had been drawn in the dirt for the wrestling. The anticipation in the air was thick with the scent of spilled mead and sweating bodies. Young boys, intent on showing their skill and proving what great warriors they would be, gathered and cheered for their friends as the bouts began.

Approaching from out of the forest, Brand watched and waited for the challenge he knew was coming. He begrudgingly appreciated that Runa gave him the warning about what Gorm had planned, but then remembered she asked him to take her away and let his sworn enemy live. Fury against her rose that she would ask him to give up his final revenge and he decided at that moment to steer clear of Runa. He cast thoughts of their night together from his mind and watched the wrestling.

A couple of hours passed while a winner was determined between the younger wrestlers. After a few hours of rest for a noon meal, the first of the older men stepped forward. The two men stripped bare to the waist, faced off and the match began. The surrounding crowd cheered for the warriors.

Brand didn't see her approach, but suddenly Signe was standing by his side as if her witchery had made her magically appear. In her hand was a horn of mead. Gooseflesh rose on his arms as Runa's warning rang in his head.

"Brand Keitelsson, you have yet to enjoy my mead. It is the best in the village, I promise you." She held the horn out to him with a smile and waited for him to take it.

Looking at the horn with suspicion, he reached out and took it with a nod of acknowledgment. Wordlessly, she watched him and seemed to be waiting for him to drink. Flynn Bloodhead approached, and Signe's attention turned from Brand to him. She turned to go to Flynn's side but looked back at Brand. Holding the horn up, Brand peered inside and remembered it would more than likely be filled with something that would make him weak and sick. He sniffed it and it smelled like fine mead and not poison.

Doubt assailed him, and he wondered if it truly was tainted, or had Runa lied to him. Then again, *why* would she lie to him? To make him forget his blood debt and leave with her? Then again, why would Signe serve him from her hand?

Runa was a silly girl with fanciful ideas. She wanted him to take her away. The night they spent in the forest was still a fresh and pleasant memory, but he began to suspect it had been part of a plan. Had she lured him with witchery on Freya's night? Was he under a spell to lay with her to draw him away from killing the old man? It was certainly not like him to take his pleasure with a woman he did not know or with any woman for that matter. He had been single-minded before meeting her and coming to this place. He had denied himself the comfort of a woman's arms until her. Now with his revenge so close at hand, she threatened to take it all away.

Brand grew even more furious with Runa as his thoughts fled down a path that led to betrayal. She was just another in a long line of people to deceive him. His greatest enemy was someone she cared for, and his trust had been misplaced once again. Guile, beauty, and seduction were her weapons used to strike a pleasureful blow. He refused to be lied to and manipulated. In a fit of defiance, he downed the mead in a few gulps until the horn was drained. The crisp honey flavor coated his tongue with sweetness but left a bitter taste behind.

#

The crowd shouted for their favorite wrestler and waived their fists, gathering around the competition as the rounds of wrestling continued. There was a bit of shoving and a few punches thrown outside the ring as well when disagreements on calls were made. This was crude wrestling and as there were few formal rules the objections went unnoticed. Brand watched it all from the back of the crowd, letting his eyes wander over the men and women gathered for this second day of the solstice festival. He finally caught sight of Gorm and his sons Vidar, Bjorn, and Vonn, standing on the other side of the ring. Vidar caressed his thick silky, dark gold beard while he watched the two wrestlers compete. Brand's stomach gave a sickly lurch.

As the ranks of contenders dwindled and one man remained victorious, Vidar stepped forward to take on the winning wrestler. The match was shorter than most and Vidar made swift work of the man, throwing him down to the ground easily. In the next bout, the other man was more cautious, and he threw Vidar to the ground. This angered Vidar so much that he attacked his opponent viciously and pinned him to the ground smashing his face into the muddy grass. There were boos and shouts of dissent that Vidar cheated, but he helped his opponent up from the trampled ground, gave him a friendly pat on the back, and shoved him away. Vidar was pronounced the winner having won two of the three rounds. Then Vidar looked out into the crowd until he found Brand's face.

Vidar pointed directly at him and roared a challenge. Brand could not refuse, or he would appear as a coward, so he pushed his way forward. He watched as Vidar's eyes dropped to the drinking horn in Brand's hand and he gave a knowing smile. Brand's skin flushed red as he tossed the empty horn away and strode into the ring that served as the wrestling arena. Vidar faced him nose to nose.

"I will break you," Vidar said.

"You can try," Brand answered with breath heavily laden with the scent of mead.

Both of them were big, muscular men. Vidar was slightly taller than Brand but not by much. They both removed their shirts which revealed Vidar's larger, softer belly. Brand was solid muscle from years of hard life and battles. Flexing his arms and rolling his shoulders, he tried to decide which bone on Vidar's body he was going to break first.

Their eyes filled with a determination to emerge victorious as Brand and Vidar stepped forward to do battle. The man serving as the referee began explaining the rules, but Vidar held a hand up cutting him off.

"This stranger is not from our village and so I declare that no rules shall apply. If he is willing or if he is a coward, he can back out now."

"The winner shall be determined by submission only," Brand said loudly.

The referee nodded once and then left the ring. Someone handed him a dripping horn of mead and he stood back to watch. The crowd pressed forward. Among them was Gorm who grinned with satisfaction that his plan was beginning to take form.

Facing off, the two warriors stood until a cattle bell clanged beginning the match. Then with a surge they grappled. Brand's one hand went around to grab the back of Vidar's neck and the other arm went around his other shoulder and locked on. Vidar executed the same grips and they each began to tug. A test of strength began as they pushed forward and then back, each straining to gain the upper hand and bring the other down.

'A leg would hurt most and cripple this bastard,' Brand thought as he strained against Vidar who grinned with confidence.

As he knew he would, Brand felt Vidar suddenly give way and step to the side. Vidar's long leg swept back toward both of Brand's legs with the intent to sweep both feet out from under him so that he would crash to the ground. In anticipation, Brand stepped wide so that Vidar missed. He pivoted on one foot and swung around until he was behind Vidar locking his head in the crook of his arm. He squeezed tight, trying for a submission. Vidar was gasping for air, spittle flying as he clawed at Brand's arm for air. Then he stamped down on Brand's foot and the second the arm was loosened the slightest bit, he lunged forward breaking the hold. After taking a few coughing breaths, he flew back into the fight.

'The sword arm would be the greatest loss.' Brand finally decided as his vision swirled.

The next few minutes of the match were a blur of grappling holds and sweeping kicks. Neither man went down. Brand fought purely on instinct as his stomach roiled. The crowd cheered every time Vidar landed a blow or got out of a tight hold. Suddenly, Vidar grew impatient, and he began to throw punches at Brand's feverish face. Fists began to land on chin and body as the two warriors exchanged blow after blow in a frenzied display of strength and skill. As the match wore on, it became clear that neither warrior was willing to back down or give up. Waves of heat flowed off Brand's chest and back, and he streamed with sweat. They broke apart after another grapple and circled each other again.

"You fight like a mare who refuses to be mounted." Vidar spat and the crowd guffawed at the crude insult.

"That's funny, you fight like you're trying to mount a mare." Brand retorted and then had the pleasure of seeing Vidar's face go bright red with anger. The men in the crowd laughed and made wagers on who would come out as the winner. They charged together.

Vidar seemed intent on breaking one of Brand's ribs and so concentrated bone-crushing blows on that area with his massive fists. Hardening his stomach muscles and bending with the blow, Brand managed to avoid serious harm, but his stomach grew sicker by the minute. One thing he learned from his years of fighting is that a desperate man, even if he is a poor fighter, can often win the fight if he were clever enough. So, he proceeded with desperation knowing the longer he could avoid serious injury the better his chances. The poisoned ale was working on him, and he swallowed frequently to keep from throwing up.

Chapter Thirteen

The crowd watched in awe as the two warriors continued to fight. Their bodies were covered in sweat and blood as they pushed themselves to the brink of exhaustion. They circled each other, searching for an opening, and a chance to strike the decisive blow that would end the match and declare a winner. It became apparent that Brand was not going to go down easily. Vidar began to kick him, trying to break a leg and he wrenched and twisted Brand's arms to try and break an arm. He seemed to get more frustrated wondering why Brand didn't go down because he was clearly sick but still managed to stay standing.

When he saw the opening he hoped for, Brand stepped in, grabbed Vidar bodily, and with a mighty heave threw him to the ground. He barely leaped out of the way of Vidar swiping his legs toward his feet. The first round of the match was over quickly, and Brand won. Vidar was livid. He surged to his feet and went to the side to rest, grabbing a horn of ale from a man's hand as he lifted it to have a drink. His nose was bleeding, and his knuckles were swollen from connecting with Brand's ribs and chin.

At the side, Brand called on all his reserves of strength, swallowed his nausea, and waited for the next round to begin. He had not managed to avoid one of

Vidar's blows and with each deep inhale, Brand's breath caught in agony. The more time that passed, the worse he felt as Signe's mead worked on his insides. He may have a cracked rib, or it might just be bruised, but his stomach churned, his head ached, and his vision was blurred. Either way, he had to end this fight, now! The cowbell rang to start.

The second round went swiftly and after grappling, Vidar managed to throw Brand to the ground. Breath whooshed from his lungs, he didn't like that at all, and his eyes swam with stars. Brand slowly climbed to his feet, and they faced off again.

"Now we finish this!" Vidar's harsh breath came in gasps, but his confidence swelled. He threw an unexpected punch that landed on Brand's mouth. His head snapped to the side, but he did not go down.

"Now I finish you!" Brand snapped back, tasting blood as his stomach revolted, infuriating him even more. He was sick from the poisoned mead, saw vengeance slipping from his fingers, and anger caused a haze in his mind. The berserker awoke and took control.

They crashed together for the last time and Brand's muscles strained against Vidar. Risking grabbing Vidar's wrist, Brand wrenched it around until it was behind Vidar's back. Then he pulled the arm upward at a painful angle. Vidar roared in pain and pulled away, which only succeeded in dislocating his shoulder. Brand let go as he felt the tell-tale pop, but he didn't give up. He threw several punches at Vidar's face letting the berserker take control and pummel his enemy. Vidar must have understood that he was about to lose because he turned to run. Brand grabbed him from behind circling an arm around Vidar's neck. Throwing him to the ground, he knelt one knee on Vidar's neck and grabbed and twisted his good arm, and pulled back. Vidar's face was ground into the muddy grass with Brand's knee crushing his neck and trying to pull his remaining arm from the socket, he shouted out his submission with a curse.

The men watching stood in amazed shock. They had not expected the fight to end this way. Gorm stormed forward and knelt beside Vidar. Brand stood, spit blood on the ground, and staggered back. He was red-faced and wanted to cast up the contents of his stomach but watched warily for anyone else to take up the fight. It took all his effort to remain standing as he fought his body to keep from embarrassing himself. Sweat poured from his skin as he gulped in air through gritted teeth as the berserker slowly retreated.

"You've broken his shoulder!" Gorm shouted at Brand after a quick examination while Vidar writhed on the ground in pain.

"Everyone heard Vidar declare there were no rules! He took the risk." Flynn Bloodhead's voice shouted as he stepped out of the crowd.

He grasped Brand's wrist and lifted his arm in the air and declared, "The winner by submission!"

Flynn's men all cheered.

Chapter Fourteen

Flynn's warriors shouted and cheered with victory. Soon men were surrounding Brand smacking him on the back with congratulations. Brand gritted his teeth as they led him away for a celebratory drink. Once he was out of Gorm's sight he waved his new-found friends off and headed toward the river to be sick.

When he reached the river's edge, Brand stuck two fingers down his throat and wretched. His stomach heaved until everything inside was out. He was hurt and ill and suddenly everything began to spin. The edge of the cool water was just within stumbling distance, and he went in boots and all. He submerged completely and felt the cold water soothe his cracked ribs and feverish skin.

Gulping down as much water as he could, he threw it up again and hoped this would rid him of any remaining mead. Then he drank as much water as he could hold as the world spun. He finally lost consciousness, splashing back into the arms of the deep river where everything went black.

#

Runa watched the fight between Brand and Vidar from the back. She was impressed with the skill with which the men fought, but she bit her lip fearing for Brand. Vidar was a bit taller, fatter, and meaner. The signs of sickness began to show about halfway through the fight and Runa knew Brand had ignored her warning and drank Signe's poison mead.

Terror struck her a hard blow and she felt every time Vidar landed a blow on Brand. The sweat pouring off him, and the sickly pallor of his face, all pointed to the poison taking control. This would ensure Gorm's plan for Brand and herself was fulfilled. Sadness swept her, and she wondered why he had not listened to her. She couldn't stand to watch anymore and, when no one was watching, she slipped away.

Runa ran down the path back to the longhouse. Everyone was at the festival except for a few thralls who were busy cooking the various dishes needed for the night's feast. Though her family treated her as one of them, they never accepted her, so they ignored her. She ran past them and said not a word as she grabbed a loaf of warm bread wrapped in a cloth. Without a word, she boldly went to her mother's storeroom of healing plants and tinctures. Grabbing everything she could think of she filled a pouch along with a small pot. Then she went to her sleeping stall and grabbed a blanket from the bed and slipped out the back. Racing back to the fight her plan played out in her mind how she would need to help Brand. If Signe had given Brand what Runa suspected, he could die from what was in that poisonous mead.

She arrived back in time to see Brand declared the winner and watched as Flynn Bloodhead raised his arm in triumph. As the men walked away to celebrate, Brand broke away from the crowd with a wave. Runa wondered if she had been wrong and Brand was not sick after all, only hurt from the fight. Doubt assailed her. Should she go after him? It dawned on her that if he had ignored her warning that meant he did not trust her. After all that had transpired between them, that is what hurt the most.

Slowing, she watched through the gaps of the gathered villagers and listened to what was going on. Signe was kneeling by Vidar's side and with a skillful twisting push, she popped the dislocated shoulder back in place. Vidar's roaring cry of pain rang out then faded to a moan. Signe was shouting orders and soon they had him on his feet. Vidar was not a man to be kept down and soon he was calling for mead to ease his pain. Gorm pulled his good arm around his son's shoulder and the crowd began to part to let them through. Runa fled before they could call on her to do anything.

Slipping lithely through the thick trees, Runa hurried and barely made it in time to see Brand fall unconscious into the river. It had taken her quite a bit of effort to catch his body as it floated on the sluggish current before he drowned. Dragging and pulling she got him onto the bank and assessed how bad his injuries were.

The poison caused his bowels to empty and so she stripped him and cleaned him up as best she could. The river mud clung to him as well. Now he shook with fever wrapped in her blanket. Death from sickness was every warrior's greatest fear. The indignation of what Gorm and Signe had tried to do to Brand, made Runa furious. Fueled by rage and resentment, the desire to thwart them rose inside her and she vowed they would not win. She would see to it.

Steeping in a pot of water over a small fire, was raspberry leaf, marigold, and a dried fruit called Idun's apples. Meadowsweet was added for healing and pain, as was the maythen plant to ease the stomach. Runa made signs over the pot and prayed to the goddess Eir, asking for healing for Brand. With a small charcoal stick, she began to inscribe the rune of healing, praying the ancient power of the runes would aid her. As she started to draw the curling bar on his forehead some force stopped her hand suddenly.

'He does not need gentleness and healing,' a woman's voice spoke in her mind for the first time in her life.

As if being taken over by a mystical power, her vision swam, and another rune appeared before her mind's eye. It swelled from a misty fog over her vision, and she saw with clarity what she must do.

The magic that took over her mind swelled as the charcoal stick drew a distinct circle with lines radiating outward and half-circle lines at the end of each main line. When the magic passed, Runa's vision cleared, and she saw the rune of power inscribed on Brand's forehead. It seemed to glow like a coal from the fire and she watched in amazement as it swelled once again and sunk into his feverish flesh. Runa understood at that moment that only magic could bring the amount of healing Brand needed. The goddess must be smiling upon them or else he might have died.

Though he was still sleeping, Brand took a deep breath and exhaled the evil Signe had tried to poison him with. A curling black smoke rose into the air and disappeared. The fever fled as well, and Brand finally slept deeply cured of evil and sickness.

Chapter Fifteen

Terror and horror captured Brand's mind. He was running through a burning house toward the sound of a woman's screams. While the walls went up in flames around him, he dreamed about the day his mother was taken from him. He recalled her face turned toward him, pale with fear as a man loomed over her taking what was not his to take. He saw the man's face gripped in the throes of ecstasy which turned to fear and pain when Brand grabbed a kitchen knife and sliced into the man. He remembered the cold, pale faces of the other men, red with anger, and saw their lips call for retribution for their fallen brother. Their laughter rang like the barking of dogs, as they looted the home and murdered Brand's father and brothers. He smelled the charred smell of wood and burning flesh and felt the cold blood on his hands. His ears buzzed and the red mist took over his brain as he tried to fight and swore revenge against the men who had murdered his family. Last, Brand saw Eiland Biersson's face furrowed with sorrow, lite by the flickering flames of the farm being burned to the ground.

The clawing sensation in Brand's guts eased slowly and the nausea that ruled him for what seemed like an age finally fled. Eyes swollen and painful, he woke from the nightmare of his past and smelled the piney vapors of smoke from a small fire. Looking down he realized he was naked wrapped in a blanket, laying on soft pine boughs somewhere in an unknown forest. His ribs had been tightly bound and the pungent scent of salve hit him. The river was close by, and the crisp smell of water refreshed him as he struggled to wake. Every blow Vidar had inflicted during the fight now made itself known again, and each deep breath verified that he had at least one cracked rib. A cut on the bottom lip of his mouth was swollen and cracked. Running his tongue over it he tasted the metallic tang of old blood. As he took stock of his aches and pains, he realized none of his injuries were bad enough to keep him from winning the upcoming fight with his enemy in…how many days? How long had he lain unconscious?

Turning his head, he saw Runa sitting next to a small fire stirring something in a pot. His stomach churned but from hunger, not sickness. He pushed up onto one elbow and stared at her wondering what to say. Only her eyes tracked his movements as she continued to stir the pot.

"Stay still. Your stomach is not yet settled, and your ribs may be broken." Ordering him, she poured a measure of hot tea and rose. In her bare feet, she brought him what she had prepared and then knelt holding out the cup.

"*Trust me*…it is only a healing tea to help your stomach and restore your strength."

The accusation in her words struck Brand as he took the cup. The sweet hot tea tasted like flowers and honey, and he sipped it while watching her rise and go back to the other side of the fire. She bent to pull on her boots and gather her things. Birds sang in a tree overhead, a slight breeze rustled the leaves, and the sound of the river flowing filled the silent space between Brand and Runa. She would not look at him while busying herself.

"I should have heeded your warning." Brand finally spoke, admitting this as an apology.

"Why didn't you listen to me?" Runa's anger flared and she glared at him. "You drank Signe's mead after I told you what they planned! You have many bruises and probably broken ribs. You almost died because you wouldn't listen to me!"

"I...thought you were trying to trick me. I thought you lied." Brand looked slightly ashamed.

"*I* was trying to trick you? Into what? I was only trying to warn you that's all. I heard what Gorm planned for you, for us *both*, and I didn't want you to get sick or be killed."

"You begged me not to kill my enemy who resides comfortably in your father's hall! He is the man who helped slaughter my family! He betrayed our trust, our hospitality, he betrayed me! He is the last of them. Nothing will stop me from killing him! Not even you!"

"I'm not trying to stop you from taking the path you have chosen. Your fate and Eiland's fate are interwoven. The future is already weaved, nothing I can do will unravel that. All I want is to escape the cruel life I have lived since the fateful night my mother lay with Flynn Bloodhead! I want to be more than a reviled mistake. I want to be treated with love, not scorn. I want to be *trusted!* My family treats me no better than one of their thralls. Flynn Bloodhead does not attempt to help me, and I am tired of it all. I've decided to stop living in fear and head down the path to my destiny. Whatever that may be. Like it or not you and I bonded Freya's night when we lay together and were blessed by the goddess to have found each other. I had hoped it meant more than just one night of pleasure. Now I see that my hopes were misplaced. You will kill Eiland Biersson when the solstice festival is over in nine more days, then you will leave, but I will not be here to watch it. I'll not continue to live in fear of beatings, reviled, hated, and forgotten. It is true, that once my heart hoped for us to go and build a life together, but I see how mistaken I was. Over the span of one day, you have made it clear that you do not trust me. Do what you will Brand Keitelsson, I'll not stop you."

Runa was in a fury. Brand wounded her heart and shattered her dreams. The beauty of their solstice night together was forever overshadowed by his lack of trust in her. He risked his life because he did not trust her and now, he feared, there was nothing left between them. Her heart was heavier than she could bear. Rising, she grabbed a half loaf of bread and walked to where Brand lay. This was all she had left, and she gave it to him. Then she retreated, grabbed her satchel, and turned.

"Drink your tea!" Her voice cracked.

Runa left disappearing into the shadows of the forest. He watched her walk away until he could no longer see the flash of her bright red hair.

The fire crackled and spit sparks. Brand sat up feeling a little lightheaded. The bread she gave him was a day old but still filled his belly. He looked around and saw the traces of what Runa had done for him. His clothes had been cleaned and mended, and she provided a warm blanket, bound his injuries, and made healing tea for him. The last thing he recalled was falling unconscious in the river. She had either pulled him out or had found him on shore, but either way, *she* had saved his life.

Chapter Sixteen

Flynn Bloodhead watched Brand Keitelsson appear suddenly out of the forest. The sun was behind him and to Flynn, it looked as if the young warrior walked right out of the sun. His hair glowed golden as if he was on fire. Even at this distance, Brand's ice-blue eyes sparked with menace. Gooseflesh rose on Flynn's back and a trickle of superstition rolled down his spine. As a boy, Flynn's Celtic mother told him tales of Lugh of the Long Arm. He was a warrior god and was known for his courage. Like Brand Keitelsson, Lugh sought revenge for the unjust death of his father. Now stalking out of the forest like that god of legend, was this man who had come to claim a blood debt and bring Flynn a chance to have his revenge.

Calling out he waved the young man over to him. He had been more than impressed with Brand's skill fighting Vidar but there had been something strange about it all. It was as if Brand was ill and held back or was not in good fighting shape, yet here he stood hale and whole and only slightly bruised. One of the men gave up his seat for Brand and he sat at Flynn's right side.

"Where have you been, my young friend? It's been almost two days since you bested Vidar. You've missed the sacrifices to the gods, some of the games, and much celebrating and feasting!" Flynn laughed good-naturedly and handed Brand a horn, pouring both of them a measure of mead.

Brand reluctantly took the horn and waited until Flynn drank first. Then he drank deep, the sweet taste reminding him of the last time he had mead. This time there was no bitter aftertaste and he relaxed only slightly.

Flynn began to tell Brand of the things he missed and the men around him joined in sharing stories. Baird of the black hair had a rare whit and told his story about how he single-handedly held the line in the game of toga-hunk. He bragged for a full quarter of an hour boasting of his strength in the tug-of-war and pulling the other team into a pit of mud. Most of the men were halfway drunk already. Brand watched and listened and though he enjoyed the camaraderie, he reminded himself repeatedly not to get involved with the friendship of these men as his blood debt would be paid in eight days and he would be gone. Thinking these thoughts led him to think of Runa and he scanned the groups of women and young girls for her bright red hair and slender form.

"You shouldn't have disappeared. Vidar has been bragging that he ran you off and declared himself the victor of the wrestling match even though everyone heard him submit. He's been cranky since you bested him." Flynn roared with laughter, but sobered quickly, "truly, where did you go these past couple of days? No one has seen you."

"I had enough of celebrating and took my rest in the forest. I only came back because I was hungry."

"Hungry for Runa." One of the older men, who was quite drunk, shouted pointing with his horn. "I saw you leap the bonfire and chase her into the woods on Freya's night."

"Is this true?" Flynn's brow drew tight, and his mouth pinched as if he were displeased.

Brand was in a bind. He did not want to anger Flynn over sleeping with his daughter and he did not want to admit that he had been with Runa. If it was because he did not wish to establish a bond with her or because he cared what Flynn and the others thought, he was not sure. This whole situation made him angry, and he regretted being pulled into joining this solstice festival. He wished he had just left the village and returned when it was over but had not because he couldn't risk Eiland Biersson escaping. By staying, he was able to keep an eye on him and bring this hunt for the last enemy, the last betrayer, to an end. Flynn had been waiting for an answer and he grew impatient while the other men fell silent. Brand just glared, not ready to answer.

"Well," Flynn began, "I have my answer then. We will speak of this…alone…at another time."

Brand nodded once and Flynn's eyes grew a little cold toward him, but as they continued carrying on, drinking, and celebrating, the conversation turned to raiding and past battles, and he returned to his jovial self.

As the day grew older, the men were called to go to the feast that had been prepared. The animals that had been sacrificed the day before, now roasted and boiled and cooked to make the feast. Nothing was wasted.

Beside Flynn, with his men who all walked a bit unsteady, Brand went to the feast. Again, the huge bonfire blazed and lit the area as the sun went down. The night noises were drowned out by singing and shouting, lutes and flutes, and drums playing lively music. Later there would be dancing and singing until the sun rose.

As they approached the fire, Brand spotted Gorm. On one side of him sat Vidar with his shoulder tightly wrapped and the arm bound against his body. He drank heavily. When Flynn, Brand, and the others came into view Vidar nudged Gorm and they all fell silent.

On the left side of Gorm sat Eiland Biersson. Brand flinched as if he had been punched. Rage filled him and he wanted to leap forward and throttle his enemy but Flynn grasped his arm and held him back, pulling him down onto a stump. Thus, he was forced to sit across the bonfire from his enemy. Brand seethed with impatience and irritation though he was glad to see that the old man was less feeble than the last time he saw him. The bandage on Eiland's leg indicated the wound was not healed completely, but in eight more days, it surely would be. Brand's eyes never left Eiland's, and the two enemies glared hatred at each other across flickering flames. The memory of a burning house also flickered in Brand's mind and, over the singing around them, he heard his dying family's screams.

The tension in the air was broken by women appearing with trenchers of food and bread to serve the men. Among them was Runa, which surprised Brand because he thought she had left the village completely. Her last words to him held a finality that made him resigned to thinking life would go on without her, but there she was. He could only guess that she had been stopped from leaving. His heart was glad she was not gone.

Runa carried a heavy pitcher of mead and went among the men serving the golden liquid. When she reached Brand, she avoided his eyes as she filled his horn, but he saw the pink blush spread across her cheeks. Because Flynn sat next to him and Gorm sat across the fire, he dared not speak to her. Something lurched in his chest with her so close and he swallowed guilt and longing. As she finished her task, Gorm shouted and Brand saw her flinch, but she straightened and turned to see what he wanted.

"Runa!" he shouted again, "give off those tasks and come and sit next to my guest, Eiland Biersson."

Eyes turned defiant, Runa hesitated, and he commanded, "Now, girl! Obey!"

Runa had no choice but to do as she was told. She handed the pitcher to another woman and went to sit by Eiland Biersson who leaned in close and whispered something to her. Brand watched as she nodded at him. Flynn tensed as Signe approached and stood next to Gorm. Her eyes were on Flynn. The company of warriors fell silent sensing, as warriors do, that something important was about to happen.

"Friends!" Gorm stood addressing the crowd and began in a loud voice. "I bring you happy tidings! Tonight, it is my great joy to announce the marriage of my only daughter! I have contracted her to…Eiland Biersson! They grew very fond of each other as she tended to his wounds. Eiland has expressed his desire to take her to wife…and I have consented! Drink and let us celebrate this happy union!"

Runa was staring at Gorm, her mouth open in wordless shock. Though she had known they made this deal in secret she could not believe he chose now to make the announcement. Eiland Biersson tipped his head back and drained his mead without acknowledging what had just been said. The golden liquid dribbled down his gray-blonde beard as he gulped. Signe stared across the fire at Flynn who stared back. Vidar burst into laughter as did

Bjorn who stood behind his father and brother. The men around them cheered the happy news.

Brand was sightless in a haze of red and his head buzzed like an upset hornet's nest. No one seemed to remember that at the end of the solstice festival, Eiland Biersson would battle Brand and die on the end of his sword.

There had been a *heitstrenging*, a solemn oath between Gorm and Brand and now, he seemed to be reneging on it or at least conveniently forgetting it. The time had not come yet and so Brand could not accuse him of being an oath breaker. He didn't care if this was the solstice feast and that it demanded peace. Why should he care if the goddess brought prosperity to these people over the next year? He was not going to be stopped any longer from claiming his revenge. Slowly, he gathered calm fury around him and made to rise.

Flynn's large hand shot out and grabbed Brand's arm, holding him down. The strength he exerted to keep him from rising was surprising. Brand looked over at Flynn who was swiftly becoming his enemy.

"Stay," Flynn growled between his teeth, "you will be known as an oath breaker if you do anything now. I ask you, Brand Keitelsson, to wait. Be glad Gorm did not have them married on the morrow. Your time will come, I will see to it."

Flynn smiled to himself as he gripped Brand's arm tightly holding him down. The solstice festival had eight days left in which Gorm had to keep his promise. By forgetting the oath with Brand Keitelsson, Gorm had as much as declared himself an oath breaker. A *heitstrenging* was a serious thing to break, and the solstice celebrating was not over yet. The warriors and people of the village would not follow a man who did not keep his word. A plan began to form in Flynn's mind. He suddenly saw a way to get rid of Gorm and take everything from him, including that which he desired most…Signe.

Chapter Seventeen

As the night dragged on, Runa sat frozen in horror over Gorm's announcement. It was true, she had known because she overheard Gorm and Eiland planning the betrothal. Now it seemed as if Gorm had been serious. Why he chose now to make this announcement was a mystery. None of it made sense to her because the plan to have Vidar hurt Brand had mostly failed. Only she and Brand knew he had indeed been sickened by Signe's potion, but only she knew it was with her help and the interference of the goddess that he now lived.

Signe herself seemed mystified that her poisoned mead had not had the desired effect on Brand the stranger. As the ruckus carried on around them, her eyes narrowed in thought. After a moment, the truth seemed to dawn on her, and she slowly turned her head to glare at Runa.

Runa quickly looked away. If her mother figured out that she helped Brand, there was no telling what she would do. Beside her Eiland carried on as if his time on earth were not short. Risking a glance across the fire she saw Brand's eyes catch the firelight, and flicker and glow like a *draugr*. The night was overly warm, but she shuddered with the cold look he gave her and, though she knew he was a man and no demon, she feared him at that moment. The anger poured off him so hot that she thought he would burst into flames. He stared at her and they held each other's gaze in a wordless conversation. She seemed to feel his rage building and she marveled at his control until she noticed Flynn Bloodhead's hand holding him in his seat. Whispering a prayer to the goddess, she looked away.

More food came and more mead was served. As everyone ate and drank. The merriment was deafening until a skald stepped forward and began to tell the ancient tales of the gods and goddesses, of famous warriors, and giants and fantastic creatures.

"Granddaughter," Eiland Biersson turned toward his betrothed. Slurring his words, he swayed, "help this drunk old man off to bed." He tried to rise but was too unsteady. They managed to get him up and he leaned heavily against Runa then draped an arm around her slim body. The pungent smell of sweat and mead wafted toward her, and Runa's stomach turned at the thought of marrying this man. Promising herself it would never happen; she rose and helped her betrothed to his feet.

Some of the men saw them leaving together and shouted rude remarks about consummating the marriage. The insults rang out and jokes about an old man's prowess in bed followed. They howled about the old man getting his sword sheathed. Runa's cheeks burned with embarrassment. Their crude jokes were not lost on her as she knew from being with Brand, about what they implied.

For his bad leg side, Eiland used a staff to help him walk. Runa smelled like the purple heather field where they first met, and he sighed with a building fondness for her. She helped him limp away from the celebration just as she had on the first day when she found him. They stumbled through the crowd and took the path alone to the longhouse. Darkness and silence fell around them as soon as they were out of sight of all the people. Suddenly, Eiland straightened, removed his weight from her shoulders, and turned to her. Casting his staff away, he grasped both of her shoulders, turned her toward him, and squeezed gently. Runa froze in alarm.

"Runa," he stood straight and spoke clearly. All signs of drunkenness vanished. "You are a beautiful young woman. Any man would be lucky to find himself betrothed to you. I cannot say that, while you tended me in my sick bed, I haven't snuck a look down your dress at your sweet, round breasts. You are tempting. I'll admit the thought of bedding you is greatly appealing but…you'd be wasted on a man like me. You and I both know I will not live past the day after the solstice festival. I will fight the boy and I will be sent to Valhalla. Do not fear the future because of your father's plans. Go now, sweet Runa. Find some happiness."

He bent and placed a lingering kiss on her lips. Runa could not believe what was happening. Once again Eiland had fooled everyone into thinking he was something he was not. He faked being drunk and got her away from the sneering, insulting men, and her cruel family. Now, he was as much as releasing her from their betrothal and admitting it was a farce. A sense of relief flooded her, and affection for him warmed the frigid blood in her veins. Eiland pulled her into a powerful embrace and then quickly released her. Turning, he strode away. His back was straight, his shoulders broad, and his limp was completely gone. At that moment, Eiland was as strong a warrior as Runa had ever seen. She wondered, was it the trickster Loki who lent his power of shapeshifting to this man? He seemed to change from old and feeble to youthful and strong in the blink of an eye. It was a sobering thought that Brand would have a real warrior to fight and not a sickly old man. Tomorrow was the fifth day of the solstice festival and one day closer to the two men she cared about, fighting to the death.

From across the fire, Brand watched Runa help a very drunk Eiland to his feet. Red mist clouded his mind, as the old man draped himself over her. Men called out crude jokes about bedding and the wedding night and he could not stop heated images rising from his memory. They limped away, his lover by his enemy's side. It was a relief to have them both gone but admittedly the old man's feebleness was a bit alarming. Brand just hoped he lived until the day after the celebration. Then, justice would be swift and merciless. The blood debt would be paid.

Lost in his anger and his lustful thoughts, Brand suddenly felt a strange sensation, it was like a calling or maybe it was the magic of the goddess controlling him. Something was pulling at him, and he looked up surveying the scene in front of him. Men were drunk, swaying, and singing battle songs, girls danced, and women flirted with the men. Gorm and Vidar participated in a contest to see who could drink more and remain conscious. Looking beside him, he noticed Flynn had left while he was lost in his thoughts. Signe was nowhere to be seen and it was obvious to him they were off somewhere together. He was the only calm within the celebratory storm surrounding him.

As the feeling became stronger Brand looked out into the night in the direction Runa and Eiland had taken. His anger flared that, not only had his enemy taken his family from him, and now, he was taking Runa, the woman he…loved? That is when he spotted her. She was standing at the edge of the clearing, just inside the trees. It was her magic that called him, and he was captured by the sight of her. Her hair was dark like blood in the shadows, her skin was pale like the moonlight on the water. He had to answer. Rising he covertly left the gathering.

As he almost reached the trees where Runa stood, she turned and walked away. This time she did not run, nor did she look back to see if he followed. She was as graceful as a doe and as beautiful as a goddess. Brand followed, his blood heating with every step, his heart pounding with excitement, and his body pulsing with need.

The magic of the night called and brought the lovers together once again. Though Runa had not thought she would ever be with Brand again, he now followed. Would he claim her? They walked far with only the moon to light the way. When they reached the safety of a private glen, she turned toward Brand and waited. He was breathing hard as if he had just run a mile. His hands clutched into fists and his eyes glittered in the silver light. As he took her in his arms the night seemed to sigh with relief.

They shared soft kisses, and he nuzzled her throat, rubbing his rough face on her soft skin. Her hands smoothed up his shoulders and laced in his hair. Runa shivered with relief that she was once again in Brand's arms. They did not speak, only shed their clothing, lowered to the dew-covered grass, and joined. This lovemaking was different, slow, and sensuous not the rushed desperate coupling as the first time. They looked into each other's eyes and undulated together, with soft touches and gentle kisses they explored the depts of passion.

To Runa, each time she was with Brand felt like a gift. Her mind overflowed with sensations and magic flowed between them. She could feel the strength in his body and was fascinated with everything about him. The caresses and the moans of delight overjoyed her, and she reveled in giving him pleasure just as she strived to seek her own. As their passion grew, he shared the warmth of his body and their hearts beat in time to the same rhythm. It would not have surprised her to discover that his blood flowed into her and hers into him. The magic of their desire, their need, and their fulfillment burst into the night and floated like mist into the sky. If the goddess watched, surely she would be pleased with the lover's offering.

After their passion cooled, they slept. Brand curled around Runa. His strong arm lay across her in a protective embrace. His body was satiated and lay exhausted, a testament to the intimacy they had just shared. The scent of her hair was comforting as he fell into a dreamless sleep. He had not felt the need to say anything or make any apologies or excuses for his actions, but he hoped that she understood.

The magic still had hold of Runa as she slept, and she dreamed with vivid clarity. Gliding through the forest cradled in dream's arms, she saw what the goddess wanted her to see. Passing through trees unhindered by the green summer forest, she came across two lovers. Flynn held Signe naked in his arms and they kissed with passionate desperation. Tears flowed down Signe's cheeks as she whispered of her sadness and how she missed Flynn. She spoke of her hopes that someday they could be together. Runa could not stand the sight of her parents together and pulled away from the scene.

The dream took her to another place toward other lovers in the throes of passion, living out their hidden desires. Suddenly, there were two more people familiar to her. Gorm and Aileen, Flynn's wife, were together. Impaling her from behind, he treated her as he did everything else, rough, and crude. Aileen cried out in pain or ecstasy it wasn't clear. Gorm finished quickly and pulled away. Aileen straightened and shoved her skirt down before turning to face Gorm.

"You will do as you promised and set your wife aside!" she demanded breathlessly.

"Yes, yes, Aileen. Give me time and I will think of a way to do it." Gorm slurred his words and swayed drunkenly.

"You oaf! That's what you said last year. Now do it or there will be no more meetings like this. You promised I'd be the Jarl's wife. You promised me her status, all her jewelry, and wealth. And get rid of her witch daughter or I swear you'll rue the day you seduced me. I will hold you to your promises! Do it or I'll tell Signe we've been meeting in secret, and I've given you what she wouldn't."

Gorm drunkenly staggered back until he bumped into a tree, he slowly slid down the bark until he hit the ground. He waived a hand at her and nodded off to sleep. Aileen whirled and left him sitting in a slump.

In her dream, Runa turned and headed back to the way she came from. She had no idea why the goddess showed her these things, but she understood that everything would be revealed in due time.

Chapter Eighteen

When she awoke, the early morning mist was lazily curling over the ground creating moving shapes and patterns. It felt as if the goddess had communicated in Runa's dreams, and she understood the message conveyed to her. Brand slept soundly and with stealth she did not know she possessed, she rose, dressed quickly, and was away without waking him. She did not know what to say to him and did not want to be caught in the awkward moments facing him would bring. They had been lovers once again and the magic of the night stayed with her as she returned to the longhouse. Gorm's announcement echoed sourly in her mind and Eiland's words and affection last night puzzled her.

As she walked, the mist swirled around her cool and wispy. The morning held a little of the magic she felt the night before. Everywhere she looked, runes presented themselves to her. In the tree branches, in the mist, in the leaves, and the clouds overhead. Her mind swam with the images, and she focused, trying to understand what the message was. Fehu for luck appeared as a tree trunk and branches. Uruz for endurance and strength appeared in fallen leave patterns. Looking up as the morning sun brightened the sky, she saw Thurisaz distinctly formed in a line of clouds. A chill ran up her spine. This was the rune of tremendous energy and seemed to be warning her to be cautious and plan her every move carefully. It also confirmed that a battle was eminent. In that, she was not surprised as she well knew Brand would fight Eiland to the death. Why it was revealed to her was puzzling, but she knew that eventually she would be forced to take a stand against ignorance and aggression. Above all, she must be strong and persevere.

Her thoughts centered around Gorm's announcement last night and Eiland's confusing actions afterward. If Gorm and Aileen were truly lovers, as her dreams revealed, then Signe was in danger. If it were danger of being displaced as Gorm's wife, then that might not be so bad because she could go be with Flynn and Runa could live with her true father as well. She hardened her heart thinking they all got what they deserved and none of it would affect the plans she had for her life.

Lost in contemplation, she did not see anyone else on the path until a large hand reached out and grabbed her arm as she strolled toward the longhouse. She was wrenched around and stared up at Gorm's angry face.

"Where are you going, you worthless wench?" Gorm snarled and squeezed her wrist.

"I, I'm on my way…I was just performing my duties." Runa bent under the pain he was inflicting on her. It felt as if her bones would snap in his grip.

"You better have performed your duties to Eiland, your future husband. If I find out you didn't bed him last night, I'll make you pay. I've had enough of your insolence; you're sulking around and your ugly face is always in my path."

"Father! Please let go you're hurting me!" Runa struggled in his grip.

Gorm would not relent. He kept hold of her as if he were gripping a sword hilt and pulled her along. They walked through the trees the rest of the way to the longhouse and then Gorm pushed open the main doors and yanked her through. Runa stumbled behind him, towed along like an errant child. When they finally reached the stall where Eiland Biersson slept Gorm ripped open the door covering and shoved her forward.

"Tell me this lazy thrall has done her duty to you last night!" Gorm thundered.

Eiland had been sitting on the edge of his sleeping box tying on his boots and now he stood. In the small sleeping stall, suddenly Runa was flung into his arms. He held her almost protectively against him and stood up to Gorm.

"I was too drunk to do anything last night except stumble to bed." He chuckled. "Runa saw me safely here and I sent her back out to enjoy the feasting. Besides we are not yet married so there is no duty owed to me." Eiland spoke calmly which seemed to deflate Gorm's anger.

"There will be no formal wedding. Last night I declared she is your wife in front of everyone in the village. Last night's solstice feast was your wedding supper, and the festival drums beat your wedding song. That is good enough. Runa is your wife now by my proclamation."

"That is not my way, Gorm. If Runa and I are to be husband and wife, then it should be done properly. Not to mention that there is the small matter of my death to come the day after the solstice festival is over. I saw the boy at the feast last night and he looked hale. You've not fulfilled your part of the bargain it seems. Until we know the outcome of the battle to come, I will wait to wed Runa only if I live past that day. I will not bring dishonor to her."

Gorm grew red in the face, and if it were possible, he grew even meaner. Runa stood with her back against Eiland's chest and didn't say a word. Though none of this was new to her, she turned and looked at Eiland with accusing eyes. He looked straight over her head and did not say a word to her. Gorm stepped forward and lowered his voice to a menacing level.

"This whore has already given her body to your enemy. Brand Keitelsson has already taken what should have been given to a husband!"

"You would not allow me to have a husband before now! Why the change of heart?" Runa spoke bravely but trembled with fear at her insolence. Gorm ignored her as if he had not heard her. He went on speaking to Eiland.

"Your enemy has had her and if you have not bedded her as we agreed and made it known, I'll have his bastard on my hands, and I simply won't have it. For now, you are under my protection, sleeping under my roof and eating my food. You agreed to take her. Bed her now to seal the marriage and let anyone who will listen, know of it. If a solstice child comes, you'll be thought of as the father. If I have to, I'll watch to be sure my wishes are carried out. Get it done! If you don't, it won't be that *draugr* who ends you. I will!"

Gorm's words rang in Runa's ears. She was shocked to learn that somehow Gorm knew of her night with Brand. Against her back, she felt Eiland take a deep breath and nod his assent. His exhaled breath stirred the hair at the top of her head and his warm arm was around her protectively. Before he left them, Gorm turned and pointed a finger at Runa.

"Take your husband to the bathing hut and see to him!" He was snarling through gritted teeth, angrier than she had ever seen him before. "Keep in mind it has been too many years since we sacrificed a human to the gods. I can bring that tradition back. Continue to defy me, girl, and you will hang from the nearest sacred tree."

#

Eiland followed Runa to the bathing hut. It was a round building with a peaked roof that had a hole in the top center to vent smoke. This was a luxury only the Jarl enjoyed, as it was built over a natural hot spring and had a cold-water brook running through it as well. Someone had been there already that morning and had set out fresh drying cloths and emptied the waste bucket. A fragrant paste of moss, juniper, and oils was in a bowl as soap for washing skin and hair. Wooden tweezers, a sharp knife for shaving, and a comb made from an antler were laid out neatly on a small table.

Eiland did not speak to Runa as they went into the building together. The sound of the bar sliding across the door and locking them in made her flinch. She eyed the shaving knife and thought, if he should force himself upon her, she would defend herself.

The idea of him being her husband without a formal ceremony and only Gorm's proclamation made at the feast last night, was horrifying. She felt ashamed. If they were truly married by law, then Runa had spent her wedding night with a man who was not her husband. She turned to face Eiland. Refusing to be forced into anything, she vowed she would fight him if she had to. She edged back toward the table with the shaving knife. He stood staring at her as if he were truly contemplating what he had to do.

Slowly, he began to undress. His woolen tunic lifted over his head and dropped to the floor. Then he bent to remove his boots. As a wife, it was Runa's duty to undress him, but she could not move, and he did not ask it of her. He only stared at her. Bending to remove britches and linen drawers he left them on the floor and as he straightened Runa could see his entirely naked body.

Eiland revealed to her he was just past his fiftieth year on the earth, but he had lived a hard life. Standing in front of her now he did not look like an old man as she had always thought of him. She only now paid attention to how tall and muscular he was, as she looked along the length of his body. Before, he always walked hunched over and limped. Now, he stood strong and formidable. He was pleasing to the eye, with a lean stomach, a broad chest covered in graying blonde hair, and long sinewy muscles. His biceps were large from a long life swinging a sword and his legs were straight with thick muscles. His skin, though scarred and a little wrinkled with age, was tanned and didn't sag. The long wound on his leg was healing nicely, though it still had green bruises and was scabbed over in places. Now, standing revealed before her, was a seasoned warrior, not a sickly old man. He stood still in front of her letting her look her fill. Runa tried not to look down at what was hanging between his legs, but from the one glimpse she had it was hard not to notice, he was large and half erect. She quickly squeezed her eyes shut but opened them back up when he spoke. Eiland took a deep breath and held his hands out wide. He seemed like a changed man. A different, stronger man.

"This is all I am Runa. All that the gods have gifted me with, all that I have left. Gorm has declared...well, you heard him, I need not repeat it. I thought of you as a granddaughter when I met you. While you took care of me, I thought of you as a friend and healer, and it is strange now to change my way of thinking and consider you as a wife. You would be a young, comely wife to be sure, and wasted on an old man like me. I tell you now, I desire you and it would not be a hardship for me to do as Gorm commands...but...I will let the choice be yours."

Eiland looked virile and young standing before her, offering himself. It was more than that, it looked as if the man standing before her now had a veil lifted and age fell from him like a discarded cloak. Despite the difference in their ages, his appeal was undeniable.

Carefully, behind her back, Runa set the knife back on the table. This man was no threat to her. She closed her eyes and pictured Brand asleep in the forest, reaching forward to remove a leaf from her hair, leaning above her undulating in a smooth rhythm with her own body. Then her head rang, remembering his harsh words.

"I do not need a wife and I have no wish to tie myself to the people who harbored my enemy and

conspired against me! I will kill that old man who betrayed me, and I will leave this place and you behind!"

Brand did not want to marry her, but Eiland did. Cheeks flushing with embarrassment, she swallowed and could not look at him.

"Ah, well, that is as it should be." He nodded at her silent rejection.

Eiland turned his back to her and strode to the hot spring. She could not help herself and looked with interest at his muscular backside as he walked to the pool. Her eyes fixated on a deep red mark shaped like an oak leaf low past his hip on the sleek plain of his backside. Eiland's birthmark signified wisdom, strength, and endurance. She nodded her head thinking deeply of the magnitude and the meaning of this mark. The sight of it was imprinted on her mind.

He laid back against the worn rock at the edge of the pool and closed his eyes, sighing with relief. Behind him, for a long time, Runa stood unsure of what she should do. Finally, she felt moved to gather bathing implements and went to tend to him as was her duty.

Carefully, she unplaited the braids on his temples, tipped his head back, and ladled hot water over his hair then scrubbed. She repeated the actions on his back and chest scrubbing with the cleansing soap then she rinsed him with clean water. She trimmed his beard a little shorter and neater and busied herself cleaning him. Eiland was silent while she tended to him and only moved when she gently pushed him to reach other places. The silence in the hut was uncomfortable but the scent of the forest's blessings was calming. Runa never knew what to expect from this man, so she remained silent as she tended to him. She did not want to admit to herself that her body was moved by him. Her cheeks flamed with guilt.

"So," Eiland broke the silence. His voice was calm but inquisitive. "You've lain with my enemy…given him the sweetness of your body."

It was a long time before Runa answered. Her face burned red with embarrassment and shyness, but she finally explained.

"It was the first night of the solstice celebration on Freya's night. I chose him, I don't know why, maybe because he was the only one who would defy my father and have me. He leaped over the bonfire for me, and we did as many maidens and warriors do on Freya's night. Before, when I came of age, my father never let me participate in the solstice festival except as one of the thralls to wait hand and foot on everyone else while they enjoyed the celebration, there was only work for me. I was determined that this time, I would defy him and so I did."

"Ah, you're a brave girl," Eiland said, as she finished scrubbing the thick firm blades of his back.

Leaning back again he closed his eyes and smiled in rapturous bliss as her hands worked on him.

Her eyes kept darting to the full erection Eiland had under the water and she was surprised when she felt her body flush with heat and moisture in response. Her breathing quickened and her hands shook. She was brave and determined to do what she wanted, not what was required of her or demanded, making her own choices made her powerful. Her heart went out to this man who was destined to die.

"Do not be afraid. Go to him. Give him comfort in his last days."

The goddess's voice spoke in her mind once again and Runa's head swam with the magic she always felt when the goddess was nearby. Before she could think about the consequences of her actions she rose, reached for the hem of her dress, and drew it over her head. Trembling, she let the cloth fall to the stones. She could not disobey the goddess and, she realized, *she* wanted to, as well.

Eiland's eyes were closed as he leaned back and enjoyed the soft firm strokes of Runa's hands. As a healthy male, the effect she had on him could not be helped, but it was not to be, and he had to keep telling himself that. Not having her was torture the more she touched him. When she moved behind him, he felt a puff of air as her dress hit the stones, and then suddenly she stepped into the pool. His eyes flew open. She was naked and glorious, and she was coming to him. His pulse leaped.

The heat of the bathing hut made her skin flush pink, and her nipples were standing erect and enticing. Her long hair fell to her waist in soft red waves and floated on the water around them. Eiland's pulse raced as she stood before him unsure. How life surprised him as he took her hand and pulled her over to straddle him. Runa was young and beautiful and the shock he felt was the biggest and most pleasant of his life. That she chose to give herself to him, a man whose life skein was short, was astonishing. This was a gift, and he took it with all the gratitude in his heart.

"Is this what you truly want?" Eiland's voice was raspy with need as he pulled her close.

"It is *my* choice." Runa's voice was firm as she looked him in the eyes.

"Then it shall be."

Eiland thrust upward and joined their bodies. Runa threw her head back at the contact and settled him deeper. He groaned and leaned forward kissing her breasts, running his hands up her slim back and down over her backside. He gave a sound like a low growl as he moved.

"By the gods!" Eiland exclaimed in wonder. "Would that I could die in your arms, Runa. I'd forego Valhalla and die happily!"

Head cast back and body yearning toward completion, Runa tried to give Eiland every pleasure she knew of. Her flesh pulsed as they loved. The warm water surged around them. Suddenly, he disengaged and stood, turning her swiftly, he positioned himself back where he had been. Now in control, his hands caressed her hips and he bucked hard and fast. Gritting his teeth as the culmination of his passion rose and could not be contained, he quickly finished.

Runa was panting, eyes wide with shock over what she had just let happen. When Eiland released his seed, she felt moved, satisfied, and pleased. The goddess surely would be delighted with what happened between them. She sighed with relief as Eiland leaned his weight against her back placing small kisses on her shoulder. His breathing was heavy but slowed as the moments ticked by. This was a different kind of silence between them but what was done, was done.

"Knowledge of this would satisfy Gorm." Eiland's voice rumbled against the back of Runa's neck.

"Yes," was all Runa could think to say. Her heart fluttered like a wild bird, and she suddenly felt a little afraid of what she had done with Eiland. What if Brand were to find out? Did she care if he did? He did not want her, and she had to remember that. She shrugged, thinking, *I must do what is best for me.*

"Not one word will fall from my lips of this gift you've given me, sweet Runa. Jarl or no, Gorm be damned."

"Thank you, Eiland." She was surprised he seemed to be reading her thoughts.

They lounged in the water without speaking to each other for a long time. There had been a great shift in their relationship and Runa was not sure how she felt. On one hand, he was quite a bit older than her, though his body was closer to that of a young man. On the other hand, though they had no blood relation at all, she had thought of him more as a grandfather figure rather than a lover. How things changed once he stood strong and attractive, and revealed that he respected her and made it her choice.

Eiland's hand caressed her breast as she leaned against him, but he made no other move toward her, nor did he seem in a hurry to leave the water.

"Tell me, Eiland, you've spoken of what happened with Brand's family before, but why did he say he saved you...killing you...for last? He spoke a little bit about it, but I'd like to hear from you about what happened. How you could...is it true you..."

"I didn't have any part in the worst of it. Let me start from the beginning. We had been shipwrecked on the shores of northern Jutland where the boy's family farm was on the headland. His father helped us repair the damage done to the ship and his mother...well, she tended our wounds and fed us, providing healing for our sicknesses. She was a good woman. It was Dursi who wanted more than she was willing to offer. He behaved himself for the most part, until the last night before we were to set sail. He'd only been biding his time. Then he decided it was now or never and took what he wanted. You know the rest, the boy found them and attacked. He butchered Dursi, carving the blood eagle into his back so fast it was inhuman. He delt the killing blow in the belly when Dursi turned to defend himself. In retaliation, my men killed the farmer and his other sons, but they couldn't catch the boy."

"But why did he say he saved you for last?" She asked again.

"Ah, yes. The ship took a long time to repair. Months in fact, but the spring turned to summer and the weather was fair. We did not mind biding our time there. The farmer was skilled in woodwork and did most of the repairs on his own. So, time passed slowly while we all healed from our wounds and sickness. Brand was an innocent young boy who was large for his age. He was impressed by the men who were like warriors from the legends, and he loved the tales we told at night by the fireside. My sword was a wonder to him, and he wanted to learn how to wield one. He followed me around like a puppy and hounded me to teach him and, as I had nothing better to do, I did. To say he was a quick learner would be to understate it. The boy was born to swing a sword and was almost as good with an axe as any man I've ever seen. He and I became fast friends though the age difference was wide, he had an old soul. So, we became sword brothers. The boy wanted to leave with me and go Viking with us, to sail the open seas and experience the glorious life of a thane, seeking riches and gathering tales to brag of our exploits."

Runa shifted against Eiland as his deep voice told her what had passed between him and Brand. Her heart ached for the friends they had been and for Brand's innocence that was shattered by his friend.

"When the men found Dursi, all cut up, with the boy standing over him with a bloody knife, they were enraged, and the carnage began. The boy's father and I were down by the shore loading supplies onto the ship. We planned to leave with the morning tide. I looked up and saw flames on the horizon. My men were running toward the ship. They said the boy had gone berserk and they feared him and ran to the ship to leave as soon as they could push the prow into the water. They cut down the farmer before I could stop them. As they boarded the ship, they kept yelling that a *draugr* was chasing them. I looked back and saw a lone figure standing on the hillside, watching us go. It was the boy. I swear, outlined by the flames of the burning farm, he glowed like Surtur rising from his Hel cave, and I could hear him shouting that he would avenge his family.

After we sailed and I found out about what Dursi did and the carnage the men had wrought…well, there was nothing I could do by then. The men had looted and burned everything and killed the people who had given us help and hospitality and had become our friends. It is no wonder, over the next ten years, the boy pursued us. He knew from the time we spent together where we were from, and he found and killed the men one by one. No matter how far we ran or how we fought back the boy was relentless. I believe he saved me for last because I was the Jarl, his friend and sword-brother, and in his eyes, I was just one of the men who killed his family. I managed to outrun him, but in the days before you found me, the boy caught up and almost ended it. That is how I got this leg wound. I escaped him then, but I am tired of running. After the solstice festival, I will fight him and one of us will die. What happened was my fault, my shame, and will be my end. Now, you know it all."

Runa listened with rapt attention as Eiland told her what happened to Brand and his family. She heard the sorrow in his voice as the events unfolded like a picture in her mind. Now she understood what the runes had been trying to tell her that morning. The choices she would be faced with and the events to come.

Turning, she kissed the tears in Eiland's eyes and stroked him until he was ready for her. She joined him again and shared the gift of her body one last time. He gave her everything he had like a man whose days were numbered. The tears that fell from her eyes were for both men, for Brand's loss, for Eiland's regret, and for fear of what was to come. When his completion reached him, she locked her legs tightly around his lean hips and held him. She said a quick prayer to the goddess as he released. Whatever the Norns weaved would come to pass and she would let fate guide her. Urd, Verdandi, and Skuld, underneath the world tree, would weave the tapestry of fate for her, for Brand, and for Eiland.

#

Gorm stood outside watching through a gap in the wooden slats of the bathing hut. He smiled with satisfaction as he watched Eiland taking Runa. Any command given by the Jarl should be carried out without question and he was pleased that his plan was put into action. He could not get rid of Runa directly or he would risk Signe's displeasure or Flynn Bloodhead's retaliation. His eyes remained fixated watching the lovers and his body stirred at the sight. How many times did he have to remind himself that she was Signe's daughter, but not *his* daughter! She was the flesh and blood of his greatest enemy. It was not wrong to lust after a girl who was of no true relation to him. He had fought this sick desire since she came into the blush of womanhood and as she grew more beautiful, his lust grew, and he hated her for it.

'By the gods,' he thought licking his lips, *'she is beautiful.'* He stared at her breasts, her lovely face tight with passion and for the hundred-thousandth time, told himself he could not have her. He thought giving her to Eiland, an old man, would douse the fire he felt, but it did not. Surprisingly, the old man was vigorous and rutted like a bull and she seemed to have no problem being with an older man.

Gorm needed the next best thing, Aileen's soft backside flashed in his mind. Sometimes, when he stared at the back of Aileen's red head, he could close his eyes and pretend it was Runa. The desire to satisfy his flesh became overpowering. Convinced that all was as he wanted, he turned away from the bath house. Thinking of Eiland inside with Runa was torture. He spit on the ground, cursing under his breath, and called her, *"Hóra!"*

Chapter Nineteen

Flynn's dissatisfaction with being second in command, second in everything, was growing. The worst part was that Gorm was the one over him. He hated Gorm and wanted everything that he had, his large hall, his wealth, his notoriety, and most of all his *wife*. Aileen was, for the most part, a decent wife, though she could be a shrew at times. She had given him four strong, redheaded sons and took care of his household, as was only right and proper. It was golden Signe his heart yearned for and now, since meeting Brand Keitelsson, he thought he saw a way to have everything he desired. He just had to wait until the solstice festival was over and see what the future held. Gorm was playing a game with Brand, Eiland, and Runa, but Flynn was determined that *he* would come out as the winner.

This was the sixth day of the solstice celebration, and more games and feasting were planned. Flynn looked around for his wife, Aileen. She had been gone since late morning and he wanted to know her whereabouts. Seeking a chance to slip away with Signe was all he thought about these days of the festival and now it seemed like the gods had smiled upon him. Signe, unfortunately, was nowhere in sight either. Out of the corner of his eye, he saw Brand appear from the woods, looking hungry and a bit angry. Here was another opportunity for Flynn, and he approached the young man.

"Brand, I would speak to you now."

He threw an arm around Brand's shoulders and guided him to a private spot near a fire whether he wanted to sit down or not. Though the day was warm, Brand wrapped his cloak about him and stared into the fire's dying ashes. Before he began, Flynn threw some logs on the fire to bring it back to life. The scent of ash and burning wood filled the space and the flames rose as they began to feed.

"I know well how the magic of the solstice can take a man's mind away and cloud his better judgment." Flynn began. "Usually, when a man of the village takes a maiden on Freya's night, he speaks to the father about a betrothal afterward, yet, you have not approached me for Runa's hand. Why?"

"I am a warrior, on a blood quest. I seek only to fulfill the vow I made to avenge my family. Eiland Biersson is the last man I have to kill. After that I will seek my fortune elsewhere, I've no wealth, no home, and no use for a wife."

"But you have a use for her body." Flynn held his voice even, but his temper threatened to flare. "What if there is a child as a result of your union?"

"You once said to me that solstice children are loved and accepted as gifts from the gods. If a child comes from the times I spent with Runa, then that is as the gods willed it and that child will be a gift. I ask you…if there comes a child…watch over it as you should have done for Runa." His heart hurt a little saying those words. He refused to think about what leaving Runa would feel like, but the thought of a child was just as painful.

Flynn didn't speak for a while. He did not miss that Brand said, *"times"* meaning the two of them had been together more than once. The other accusation in Brand's words bit like a viper.

"Runa was indeed a solstice child and I have not done right by her all these years. She is my only child with Signe, and I do love her in my way, but Gorm is Jarl and he claimed her as his daughter. The law was on his side. Had he not, Signe's unfaithfulness would have been revealed because she was a married woman when we went into the woods that first Freya's night. Unless someone challenges Gorm she will remain under his control."

"Then you should challenge him. Kill Gorm. Take his wife and protect Runa as you should have done as her father. Why involve me?"

"I would challenge Gorm, but I don't know how Signe would feel about that. She believes she is fated to be the Jarl's wife. Aileen would be furious if I set her aside. It is a possibility to have two wives, but Signe would want to be the first wife as would Aileen, and well, women are complicated. Then there are his sons to deal with. Vidar would claim to be Jarl in Gorm's place and then I'd have to kill him too. It can all be done, but I need to figure out how to manage the ugly consequences and avoid a civil war between Gorm's warriors and mine. If I'm to have a village to rule, we can't kill each other off."

"You know Aileen goes into the forest with Gorm when you are with Signe. You four have weaved a tangled skein and now you seek to disentangle it all."

Across the glen, women worked around cookfires, and Runa was with them. Her hair was wet, and her brow was furrowed as if she were in deep thought. Brand watched as distracted, she bumped into another woman. That woman turned to berate Runa and she jumped back before the woman could strike her. As she did, she stepped on the foot of another woman who screamed at her for her clumsiness. Signe approached and after learning what was happening, slapped Runa hard across the face for not watching where she was going. Brand's chest burned with anger as Runa's head snapped to the side with the slap. Cheek reddening, she looked up and found Brand's eyes upon her, and she bravely blinked back the tears and then went about her business.

"They treat her no better than a thrall!" Brand growled.

Flynn watched Brand as the scene unfolded and saw the emotions flicker over the young man's face. He, himself, was unable to interfere with a mother disciplining her daughter, but he flinched at the sound of the slap. Once he was Jarl, Runa's mistreatment would come to an end, he promised himself. Now was his opportunity to set events in motion to make that hope a reality.

"I see you Brand Keitelsson. When you look at Runa, there is more for her in your eyes than simple lust. A man can slake his hunger within a woman's body, but he walks away with more than just bodily satisfaction. His heart is now involved. Why can you not fulfill your vow of revenge against Eiland Biersson and then make your home here in Lyngmarker? You can marry Runa and the two of you can have a place in my house. You will earn a great reputation as a fearsome warrior and an honorable man who stands by his word. With you as my son-in-law and one of my thanes, I will challenge Gorm, we'll kill his sons and take everything he owns as it should be. I will be Jarl, you will be my second in command and I'll throw in one-quarter of his treasure as your share, and Runa will be yours."

Brand tore his eyes from Runa's retreating back and slowly turned his head to look at Flynn. He could hardly believe his ears. Flynn was trying to embroil him in a scheme to take the leadership from Gorm. Brand had not a care for the man, but he did have a problem with killing a family for gain. The only part that he hated to admit had any appeal were Flynn's last words, *"Runa will be yours."*

"Have you any feelings for my daughter or is your heart only filled with revenge and hatred?" Flynn probed when Brand did not answer.

"If my life were different, I would let nothing stop me from making her mine." Brand finally admitted.

"Then it is settled. When I make my move against Gorm, you support me and in return, I will give you my only daughter as wife."

"You forget, Gorm gave her to Eiland Biersson last night. They are betrothed and she did not protest. How do you know she wants me?"

"Betrothed is not married. She'd be foolish not to want you Brand. Remember, she chose you on Freya's night. I've no doubt she worked her magic on you, just as her mother does on me. At the end of the solstice festival, you will kill Eiland Biersson. Though, you need to fight better against that old man than when you wrestled against Vidar. I was surprised you won. You were sloppy and seemed unbalanced."

"Signe gave me poisoned mead before the match. I was sick for a whole day and a half afterward. It was Runa who nursed me back to health."

"No," Flynn chopped his hand through the air. "I don't believe Signe would be capable of such a cruel, dishonorable thing. You are mistaken."

"She did. It was part of a plan between Eiland Biersson and Gorm to make me weak before the fight so that Eiland could kill me. Vidar was supposed to wound me wrestling, only he failed. In the end, I was the stronger man and prevailed. Runa tried to warn me, but I wouldn't listen, that is how I know what Signe did and what Gorm planned. It was she, Runa, who healed me of the poison, and I should have believed her."

Flynn sat in shocked silence and swore under his breath. After a while, other men started to arrive. Some of Gorm's thanes were coming within earshot. He took a deep breath and leaned toward Brand; in a quiet voice, he made his final position clear.

"Leave Gorm and Signe to me. You will do the honorable thing and marry Runa in the days after the solstice celebration. All you have to do is kill Eiland Biersson."

"Aye, I will." Brand nodded.

Chapter Twenty

After the altercation with Ida, her mother, and the other women by the cooking fires, Runa fled. Tears streaming down her face, she ran through the trees seeking a solitary place to hide. As always, her steps led her to the fields of heather outside the village. They were in full summer bloom and the round bushes spread off into the horizon. Once her lungs began begging for air from running so fast, she knelt to catch her breath. Laying back among the lavender and green stalks she stared up at the sky. No solace was to be found this time and the youthful feelings that always filled her with joy and freedom in this beautiful place failed to emerge.

For the first time, she wondered why the goddess had been speaking to her these last days. If she planned to strengthen Runa or prepare her for something, it seemed to be failing. Her heart was torn. She had intended to take a lover and find a husband on Freya's night at the solstice celebration, and she had. She defied Gorm and her mother. Now, she had taken another lover and the two were bitter enemies. Runa was caught between them. One was a young, vigorous lover whose heart was grieving and full of vengeance. The other was older and though still virile, his heart had given up on life. Why she had given herself to them both was beyond her understanding. She wanted to fulfill her dreams of traveling the world with a husband as a companion and escape this harsh life.

Brand's wounded heart cried out to hers in unity and they seemed to complete each other. With him, she could have the future she desired.

Eiland had touched her heart with his kindness. He took her imagination to many places in his stories and filled her heart with hopeful possibilities. He was gentle and compassionate, and he stood up to Gorm on her behalf. If she gave into Gorm's plan and went away with Eiland as a wife, she could obtain the same things, leave the village of Lyngmarker, and start a new life away from her mother and all the ill-treatment she endured from everyone in the hall. She had thought of him as a frail old man and a grandfather figure, but her feelings changed when he gave her the gift of choice in the bathing house. Everyone in the village was fooled into thinking he was frail and wounded. What did that say about his honor? When it came time for the two enemies to fight, a strong, capable, seasoned warrior would go into battle. Eiland was destined to die on the end of Brand's sword.

Soon the two of them would come together with swords thirsting for lifeblood. A blood debt needed to be paid and a heart healed. A blood debt was owed and the only currency that could be paid was with a life. Which of them did she love? Or did she love both men?

Runa knew from having lain with both of them that they were each strong and capable warriors. Brand had youth and honor on his side. Eiland had experience and tenderness that made Runa's cheeks flush. Who would prevail in a battle to the death was up to the weaving of the Norns.

At the base of it all, in Runa's heart and mind, she just wanted to feel loved, but she only felt lost. Rising to her knees she pulled a small pouch from around her neck. Holding it in her hands she closed her eyes, took a deep breath, and rocked back and forth. Words she had heard her mother sing came to mind and she tried to call on the solstice magic she had felt growing inside her these last days. When she felt it was time, she opened the pouch and cast all twenty-four rune stones into the dirt.

The stones fell silent with the rune side down and only three were rune side up. Runa tried to pay attention to what was being revealed. One rune was Nauthiz, and it seemed to whisper Brand's name. It told her his life was out of balance and that barriers and hurdles impeded his progress. The other rune was Asch, the same rune of strength and protection Signe had drawn on Eiland's forehead to remind him of his warrior's spirit. The third was Tiwaz, the warrior's rune. Courage, strength, and bravery came with this rune and as Runa listened, the wind spoke her name.

Runa's temper flamed. These worthless stones told her nothing she did not already know and in a fit of rage, she scattered the stones with a stroke of her hand. Rising to her feet, she decided to make her own way and no gods, goddesses, or men would tell her what to do. As she stood, chest heaving with anger, Runa felt a flood of power surge through her. She looked up and screamed in anger. A flash of the sun behind the clouds swirled, looking like the goddess smiling down on her. Filled with purpose and the goddess' power, she turned and strode confidently back to the longhouse.

#

Today was the seventh day of the solstice celebration. Many people had been in the fields to harvest early vegetables. Baskets overflowed with cabbages, onions, leeks, juniper, and feathery stalks of dilla seed. Tomorrow was the planting of rye, barley, and oats to be harvested in late summer or fall. The time of the solstice celebration was the perfect beginning for summer planting as the goddess was among them to bring fertility to the land.

Keeping her distance from the other women, Runa filled her basket. She worked hard to keep her mind off the fact that in five days the solstice celebration would be over. The sacredness of the day would pass and the edict for peace would be over, and the inevitable fight between the two men she loved, would happen.

Brand approached her and gently took the basket she was carrying from her hands. She looked up into his bright blue eyes and tried to assess her feelings for him. Was it practical that she could love him only after a short time getting to know him? How could she lie with Eiland if she loved Brand? Practicality pushed aside, she could not help admitting she was overjoyed to see him. He was staring down at her, and she looked up at him, caught in a moment where the two of them inwardly rejoiced at being together. Realizing they were just standing there staring at each other among the vegetables, she moved along. The task of harvesting dilla was always one of the worst jobs. All the bending, straightening, repeatedly, and moving along with the basket was hard work in the hot sun. Thus, it was always a task given to Runa. Regardless, she was always careful not to damage the plant, so that it would grow again. The herb could soothe a baby's gassy belly, so it was prized among new mothers. Bending, she cut the flowering dilla stalks at the stem with her sharp knife. She placed it in the basket Brand held and moved on to the next bundle.

"Runa," Brand began, "I want to…well…I want to say I am sorry that I didn't trust you about Signe and I should have."

"Yes, you should have, or you wouldn't have almost lost to Vidar and gotten deathly sick. I understand why you think I lied, but I wouldn't do that to you."

"Runa, I spoke to Flynn Bloodhead about you. He is your blood father and he and I agreed, after I kill the old man, we decided that you and I will wed. I will make

Lyngmarker my home. I, *we* will live under Flynn's roof, and I will become one of his thanes."

Brand conveniently did not mention the plan to kill Gorm and his sons. He still was not sure how it was all going to play out and so it did not need to be said. He wanted no part in that particular part of a Norseman's life. Runa shielded her eyes from the sun with her hand and looked up at him.

"You've both decided, have you? And not a word to me? You didn't think about asking what I want?"

"I thought since we…are you saying you want to be Eiland Biersson's wife as Gorm declared?" Brand tried hard to keep his temper from flaring.

"I'm saying no such thing. I only want to be given a choice!"

Brand nodded, relieved.

"So, you still want to kill that poor old man?" She blushed knowing he was anything but an old man.

"I do. I will." Brand answered.

Runa's heart ached and she realized she would never talk him out of killing Eiland Biersson. It was his path and his destiny to finish what he started in avenging his family's deaths. He had to do it for his honor and his sanity. His heart would never rest if he did not silence the demons screaming for vengeance in his head. Runa turned away, bent, cut the stalks of dilla, and moved on.

"You must do what you must do. It is your path." Runa spoke listlessly and tried not to give away her feelings.

"You care for that old man?" Brand had not missed the sadness in her voice.

"Do you love me, Brand?" Runa countered.

"There is too much hate in my heart to love anyone, but once that hatred has been released, I hope to find the ability to love you."

"Brand, I can only be honest with you, *if* we marry, I want to leave this place. I hate it here and don't want to stay even if we live under Flynn Bloodhead's roof. I want to see the world and learn to swing a sword. I want to sing battle songs and swim in the sea. I would like to be by your side, but I don't want that life to begin with the death of my only friend, a man who was your friend once as well."

"Eiland Biersson is not my *friend*, he is my enemy, the last enemy that stands in my way of keeping my word to my family and laying their spirits to rest. Do not ask it of me to let him live because I cannot do it!"

"I will not ask it of you because I know it is what you must do. I only wish for there to be no...*secrets* between us." Runa's blood turned cold as she lied because she knew one very big secret that she would never reveal or repeat. Brand must never know she had been with Eiland.

"Then it is settled. We will leave Lyngmarker together *after* I kill my enemy."

With those bitter words, Brand bent and kissed Runa gently on the lips, lingering there for a sweet moment. She knew in her heart she was making the right choice, but it wounded her heart while she did it.

Chapter Twenty-one

The summer harvesting of the early vegetables and the planting of the grains commenced for two more days. Herbs were drying and meat and fish were hung in the smokehouses. Most importantly, vast kegs of mead were being brewed. At night a feast was held, and the celebration raged. Runa snuck off with Brand at every opportunity and she stayed away from the longhouse, trying to avoid seeing Eiland Biersson. Her choice was made, and she embraced it.

The people of the village never seemed to grow tired of feasting, drinking, and making merry. Arm wrestling, axe throwing and dancing were constant sources of entertainment. Runa enjoyed them all because it was what she wanted to do. With her newfound power and resolution, fear and uncertainty left. She spoke as little as possible with her mother, and her brothers, and definitely steered wide of Gorm.

She noticed most of the women of Flynn's house began to befriend her, all except Aileen, who scowled at her. Though her heart soared at this acceptance it did not change her resolve to leave. On the fringes of every feast and dance there lurked Eiland Biersson. He sat with his leg propped up and drank himself into oblivion every night. His eyes burned as he watched her dance. Every time Gorm tried to catch Runa and chastise her for not

SOLSTICE CHILD

tending to her husband by declaration, Eiland distracted him with stories and legends of old or challenged him to a drinking contest which was something Gorm never refused.

Signe watched Runa from the shadows and her rage grew. She knew everything that Gorm planned and knew that Runa had given herself to the stranger Brand, and Eiland Biersson, seemingly to obey Gorm's commands. Yet the girl flaunted her affection for a man not of Gorm's choosing. It was not like Runa to be so openly disobedient, but everyone accounted it to the solstice festival. Keeping the sacred peace was mandated by the goddess and so Signe held her tongue. Assuring herself that once the twelve days were over, Runa would be back under Signe's thumb. She turned away, planning retribution. Gorm and Eiland Biersson were drunk and broke into a song about an ancient battle. She rolled her eyes and went to find Flynn.

Later that night, hunched and moving slowly, Eiland Biersson leaned heavily on his staff as he made his way back to the longhouse. He was not far enough out of sight to abandon his fake frailty, so he continued on his way moving slowly, stumbling occasionally in case anyone happened to look. Just before he gave up his act and threw away the stick he was using, a large figure melted out of the shadows. Suddenly, Brand Keitelsson stood in front of him. His eyes gleamed red, catching the distant firelight behind them.

"Only three more days old man and I send you to Valhalla."

"Taunting an old warrior with his death is a worthless endeavor. At my age, I welcome the prospect of feasting with my old friends in Odin's hall."

"That is assuming you die with a sword in your hand and the Valkyries find you worthy to enter Valhalla, which I doubt will happen."

"Once, Brand Keitelsson, you and I were friends. You were a young boy and I taught you how to use a sword and shield. Can we bury the axe and let go of this desire for vengeance? I wasn't even at the house when my men attacked your family. I did order Dursi to leave your mother alone and he disobeyed, to his detriment. He got what he deserved as did the others, but I was not there, and I was not involved in your family's deaths."

"You were the Jarl and were responsible for the actions of your men. Those acts of dishonor fall directly upon your head! I will take that head soon. Do not drink yourself to death before I have my revenge."

"Brand, you will always be the son of my heart. I tell you hatred has a way of eating a man alive. Even after you kill me and the blood debt is paid, you will remember the friendship that was once between us. It will come back to haunt you. I ask you to save your spirit from the stain of any more death and destruction. Nineteen dead men should be enough to pay the debt. I am innocent in this war you've brought. I urge you to take Runa from this place, now, tonight while Gorm lays with a woman who is not his wife and Signe lays with a man who is not her husband. Leave and do not look back, for this is not the place for either of you. Live, love, and have children. Be happy together for the rest of your days. There is a good man inside you buried under the pain and grief. Killing me will not let him out. Let Runa heal you as she has healed me."

Brand just glared at him with narrowed eyes. There was a chill in his voice as he spoke his final words.

"Rest up, old man. Look for me in three days, and I put *you* to rest, *forever!*"

#

Runa waited for Brand to come to her in the place they thought of as their own. It was far from the prying eyes of the village people. Sleeping in stolen blankets from the longhouse, here they could be together under the stars and waning moon. The peace of the thriving forest embraced them, and the wind celebrated their love.

Tonight, guilt assailed her, and she thought about once again entreating Brand to give up his desire to kill Eiland Biersson. Whenever she mentioned it, he flew into a rage, and she feared him in those moments. Not that she felt he would hurt her, but that his spirit would never be healed. When she cast the runes, the message was clear that he was out of balance within himself and that there was no turning back if he stayed on the path he had chosen. He was a warrior and warriors fight, that was the way of the world, but would fulfilling his vow release the blackness in his soul?

Finally, Brand returned. He was in a fury and when he came upon her, he paced the glen and would not look at her.

"Brand, has something happened? Did Gorm confront you?"

"No, I…" Brand ran his fingers through his long hair and continued to stride back and forth. "I spoke to Eiland Biersson."

Runa flinched and then froze. Wondering if Eiland had told Brand about what they did in the bathhouse.

"What did he say to you?" Runa asked carefully while rising to her feet. She would not run if Brand was angry with her. If he knew she had given Eiland her body, then she would face up to the consequences. She would no longer cower in the face of fear. Her chin rose and she repeated her question.

"What did he say to you?"

"He asked me to let him go! He reminded me we had been friends once, my teacher and my mentor, a man who taught me to swing a sword and defend with a shield, the man who commanded the men who killed my mother and my family!"

"Eiland told me he was on his ship when everything happened. He wasn't there and did not command them to act as they did." Runa said gently, "Killing him will not bring them back."

"But if he was there…he could have stopped them!" Brand shouted, grabbing his head in both hands, he fell to his knees groaning with anguish. "I can still hear their screams and see the dead bodies of my brothers. It will not stop or go away until the last man responsible is dead!"

Runa suddenly understood that it was not what Eiland Biersson had done, but what he had not done, and that was why Brand hated him above all the others. He had trusted the man, had liked him, and admired him. Brand saved killing Eiland last as a punishment for not being there to stop what had been done to his family.

She went to him and knelt beside him. She wrapped her arms around Brand, holding him until his body stopped shaking with anger and grief.

Chapter Twenty-two

The longhouse was quiet and empty when Runa returned at midday to fetch her things. It was the last day of the solstice celebration and by nightfall on the morrow, she and Brand would be leaving. She did not have much in the way of belongings to take but realized there were a few things she would need and of course, she would need a satchel for healing plants and salves. No matter what happened between Brand and Eiland in the fight to come, Runa was going to leave. Gorm and Signe would surely try and stop her and so she was going to prepare to escape in secret. The question remained would she leave with Brand or Eiland? The answer was yet to be determined.

Lost in making her plans, she did not notice she was not as alone as she thought. Ida stepped from around one of the large pillars in the hall and grabbed a hand full of Runa's hair yanking her backward. This was Ida's usual tactic and Runa was ready for it this time. Clenching her fists, she turned quickly and swung. Her fist landed squarely on Ida's nose. Not expecting her victim to fight back the other woman cried out, her nose bled, and her eyes watered in shock. Runa lunged forward and grabbed Ida by the braids and pushed her face into the wall, splinters jabbed into her cheek. It happened so fast that both women were caught off guard by Runa's ferocity.

"Touch me again, Ida," Runa let her fury take hold and she grabbed for the small knife at her belt, holding it to the woman's throat, "and I'll slit your throat. I'm sick of your cruelty and you should know, I'm no longer going to take it."

Ida's face was pressed against the wall and blood ran into her mouth, turning her teeth red.

"Just wait until Gorm hears about this!" She hissed.

"Tell him if you will. I don't care but be forewarned. You see, I no longer care what happens to me here and one day it will be me jumping out at you. My knife might just find its way into your soft belly."

Runa felt Ida begin to shake with fear. She gave her a final shove and warned before leaving, "Please, keep pushing me Ida, because the next time you do, it will be the day I end you."

#

Tonight, was the final solstice feast and an end to the celebration for another year. Life would return to normal, so the people of Lyngmarker made this night the most festive. As tradition demanded, a massive boar roasted above a huge fire and the succulent scent mixed with wood smoke and herbs filled the air. Drums beat the hot night and music flowed in jaunty rhythms. People sang and danced around the bonfire until the late hours of the night and the mead flowed. The skald told stories and a filthy half-dressed priest went among the people casting blessings and making prophecies about the coming year. In groups, surrounding other small fires, sat the thanes talking and laughing and planning summer adventures. Gorm's men gathered on one side of the huge clearing and Flynn's men on the other. Though they drank and laughed tensions began to mount and the warriors grew bored with forced peace.

Brand had gone into the woods to prepare for the fight that he had waited twelve long days and ten endless years for. He would not eat or drink or lie with Runa tonight so that his strength would be at its greatest and his spirit would be powerful and ready for what he was going to do.

Runa was alone. She refused to stay in the empty longhouse and something about the magic of this night called to her. Enticed by the drums and hypnotized by the flames, she decided to take the chance and join the other women dancing, setting her spirit free. The goddess filled her with power once again. The warm night caused her skin to glisten with sweat and as she moved, the cloth of her thin dress clung to her skin.

On the other side of the fire, Eiland watched Runa, mesmerized by the movements of her slim body. The firelight reflected on her red hair and made her glow like the brightest flame among dull coals. When he first arrived at Lyngmarker, in his feverish delirium he called her granddaughter, but she was in actuality, no such relation. His mind changed over the days she tended to him, and he came to think of her as a young friend and skillful healer. The fateful night Gorm declared she was his wife, changed everything even further, and now, watching her dance with the other young women, he could only think of her as the wife he never had. He could not forget the gift she gave him in the bathhouse. The difference in their ages had not mattered then and tonight, he craved for more of her. His body ached with need and his blood rushed through his veins like molten fire, but it was not to be. He shook his head thinking of the fickleness of the mind and heart, and fate's cruelty weaved by uncaring Norns.

Eiland Biersson accepted his destiny. He had no wish to drink tonight or even pretend to be drunk. The weight of his fate bent his shoulders as he rose and covertly left the celebration. Returning to his sleeping stall in the longhouse was all he wished to do. Watching Runa was torture because he knew she would never be his. He rose to leave. A good night's rest and a clear head would help him fight skillfully when Brand came for him. All that was left was this last lonely night and the best he could hope for was to die bravely on the morrow. Though the thought was a restless beast inside his heart that now he had someone to live for, and that someone danced like the brightest flame within the fire of his heart...*Runa.*

#

Gorm's nerves were frayed and the mead he drank soured his stomach. He could not help but notice the division of men around the fires that night. He counted fifty-five loyal thanes among his followers with five more on the watch. Any worthy Jarl would have at least sixty men in his ranks, but Gorm wanted more. On Flynn's side, there were sixty, including his four red-headed sons, three of whom were old enough to fight. The disloyalty of that sixty, siding with his rival, was like a thorn in his side. Brand Keitelsson was a lone wolf, an outsider but Gorm was certain in a battle he would take Flynn's side. As they spent so much time together it was assured, the boy would not support Gorm. Why he was thinking of battle and strategizing against Flynn was puzzling, but he had an itch and his sword hand clenched. Maybe it was Loki whispering conspiracies in his ear again and making trouble. Still, there was something in the air and his shrewd eyes surveyed everyone and everything. Of one thing he was certain, the goddess Freya was leaving now that her worship waned with the celebration and Odin, the god of war, approached.

Flynn was in a tense mood. He saw his fate racing toward him on a swift wind and he longed to embrace it. His fortune awaited. This would be the last night he and

Signe could be together, then if plans did not go forward as he hoped, it would be another long year until he could be with her again. He was tired of using the solstice festival as an excuse to be with her. The cold winter would come, and he would have to withstand the sight of her at Gorm's side for another year. His flesh would ache for her body and his mouth would water for the taste of her lips, and the feel of her soft skin. Consoling himself that on the morning of Brand's fight with Eiland Biersson, all would be decided. He would call out Gorm as an oath breaker and disgrace his sons with the taint then take over as Jarl of Lyngmarker. There might be a battle, and Flynn hoped there would be. He was confident in his men and wished to wipe out any dissension right from the start. Gorm was not well-liked, and Flynn knew the people would no longer support him. It would fall naturally into place. Everything of Gorms, from the ten long ships mired at the river's edge to the longhouse, all his treasure and his wife, would all be Flynn's. Smiling, he rose to go and lure Signe away for one more embrace on this, the last solstice night.

#

The dancing made Runa feel light and free. The presence of the goddess surged within her, through and around her. Some of the other women pulled her toward the mead casks and they quenched the thirst built from vigorous play. Laughing and carrying on as one of the girls, she finally felt a little accepted and wished the night would never end. Sipping her mead, she thought of Brand alone in the forest preparing to kill Eiland. The thought of Eiland made her heart heavy and she wondered where he was. The laughing died as other women suddenly fell silent, and Runa felt a looming presence behind her. Slowly turning, she found Gorm, Vidar, Bjorn, Vonn, and Ida. Her face was puffy and red, both eyes were purple, and her nose was swollen and most likely broken. Runa's stomach lurched. This could not be good. Straightening her shoulders, she placed her mead cup down and faced them.

"What happened to Ida's face?" Gorm crossed his arms over his chest and glared at her.

Speaking right to Ida who was hiding behind Gorm, Runa shrugged.

"How should I know? I think she was just born that ugly."

Ida gasped at the insult. Behind Runa, some of the girls burst into giggles and laughter. Bjorn struggled to suppress a smile. Gorm just scowled.

"Insolent girl! You should be with your husband, not acting the Hóra and dancing like a maiden around the fires but I will deal with you later. For now, your brothers will see you home. Get you gone!" Gorm commanded and waved the three brothers forward.

Runa felt a chill trickle down her spine wondering why Gorm felt she needed an escort of three men to take her home. Vonn reached forward and grabbed her arm pulling her away from the group of her new friends. It looked as if she had no choice in the matter. Straightening her back she left with as much dignity as she could muster.

Silently, they led her back to the longhouse. Torches were lit outside the front of the hall and the flickering flames caused the shadows to make the carvings dance. It was eerily quiet, and Runa wished she could escape. Vidar and Bjorn were a few steps behind speaking together in low voices and Vonn squeezed her arm painfully if she dragged her feet. Upon reaching the doors, he pushed her inside.

"Do yourself a favor and stay inside until morning. Father is not pleased with you, and neither are we. You've earned severe punishment for how you've acted the last twelve days. I'm not happy to leave drinking to serve as your personal guard. If I see you out again before morning, you won't live to regret all you've done."

Runa flinched as they slammed the doors shut. The fire was low in the long hearth trailing down the center of the room and indeed no one else was around. Everyone was still enjoying the feast except her. She was indeed alone.

The sound of movement coming from the back startled her. Runa knew that Ida was still at the bonfire as she had watched her go and sit with a few of the other women as she was taken away by her brothers. It could not be her waiting to ambush her again. Just in case, Runa drew her knife and crept forward. A surge of energy swept through her as she moved toward the sound that was coming from the sleeping stalls. Closing her eyes, Runa knew who it was. She braced herself, not sure if she should be relieved or alarmed. Walking toward the back, approaching the sleeping stall she knew well, she reached a hand forward and slowly drew the covering back. There was Eiland Biersson.

Chapter Twenty-three

Eiland stood slowly and stared at Runa as if his thoughts had caused her to materialize right in front of him. She was holding a knife in her hand and his eyes went wide. Quickly sheathing it in the leather by her side, Runa looked relieved as she stepped in and let the door covering behind her fall. The room was close and warm, and nervous perspiration started on her forehead. Eiland somehow looked as cool as melting snow.

"Runa? Why are you here?" Eiland asked.

"I…my father banished me from the feast and sent me home. I broke Ida's nose today and am to be severely punished tomorrow for striking her." She held up her small fist and showed him a small bruise on the back of her hand that resulted from hitting the woman.

"What did Ida do to deserve such treatment?" Eiland reached for her hand and examined the small purple blotch.

"I had enough of her cruelty toward me and I hit her in the face. I think it is an improvement." Runa shrugged her shoulder and gave him a little smile.

They laughed a little at Runa's joke, but then they fell silent. Eiland was holding her hand, looking at her with longing in his eyes and it broke her heart.

"Where is…" he began.

"He prepares for tomorrow in the forest alone." She answered his question before he could say Brand's name then went on after the span of three breaths.

"I should go. Good night, Eiland." Runa turned to go, but he kept holding her hand and pulled her back.

"Stay Runa. Love me tonight one last time?"

Runa looked up into his sun-worn face and examined the lines that appeared when he smiled. His eyes were clear blue and stormy with need. Once again, the strong warrior stood before her. Runa swallowed and closed her eyes. Indecision tore at her, and it rang over and over in her mind that Eiland was soon to be killed and that she loved the man who was going to do it. Her chest ached with sorrow as she realized she loved this man who was going to die. How was it possible to love two men? He pulled her into his arms and just held her as tears flowed down her cheeks.

She felt Eiland shift, lifting her dress off her he undressed her slowly, then she stood completely bare in front of him. The candlelight illuminated her skin and the red hair flowing long over her breasts. Running his rough hands over her smooth skin his eyes glittered with need. He lowered her to the bed and stripped. His long body eased between her legs, her arms reached up to embrace him and his mouth sought hers. Hungrily he kissed her lips, her cheeks, her neck, and down to her breasts. He reveled in the salty taste of her skin as he moved slowly in unison with her body. Runa cried softly as they made love. Each time Eiland almost reached his completion, he would stop, breathe deeply, and wait until it passed and then he would start again. He made their moments together last, and he showed her ways of loving that she had never experienced before. When finally, he could not hold off any longer, tightly pressed inside her, he released, pumping his seed into her womb with a satisfied groan. Runa wrapped her legs around his lean hips and let her tears of sorrow flow. He caressed her breasts one last time and kissed her long and slowly before sliding beside her.

Eiland began to talk to her, weaving a story where they lived together on a farm and raised redheaded children. He spoke of how their days together would be and how their nights would be spent in loving embraces. He told her how proud he would be to have a young, beautiful, clever wife such as Runa would have been. He spoke until his voice was hoarse and he drifted off to sleep.

As Eiland slept, Runa swallowed her sorrow and slipped away in the early morning hours.

#

Brand's blood sang as he woke alone in the forest, covered in morning dew and anxious to begin this day, the first thing he did was miss Runa. He told her he wanted to be alone, but now he realized he truly wished she was there with him. After a long night of prayers and sacrificing to the gods and contemplating the battle ahead, he felt ready.

He sat cross-legged facing the sunrise. Rubbing an oiled cloth over his sharp sword he watched the river flow slowly by. He felt the spirits of his parents and his brothers with him, and he quivered with a need to finally put it all to rest. They seemed to whisper that they longed for peace, and he would give it to them. For ten long years, he hunted the men responsible for taking everything from him. Ten long years of hardship, chasing, fighting, and killing would now culminate in one final battle. Each man that fell to his anger assured him he was one more step closer to the peace he also sought. Thinking of Flynn Bloodhead's words that it was the way of the Norsemen to fight and take what they needed to build wealth, reputation, and for survival, he sighed. He didn't care. The last man would fall today, and Brand would be free.

Eiland Biersson, the name was like a hornet's sting in his mind. His heart shrank from it. Visions of Brand's days as a youth came unwelcome to his memory. Eiland had taught him to use a sword, he spoke of the way of the Norse warrior and filled Brand's head with stories of the gods and giants, of famous men, great deeds, honor, and tantalizing women. Brand had once admired him and wanted to be like him. They had been friends. Back then, he wanted the glory of a Viking life, but his youth was stolen from him and now he was nothing, but a hunter, a killer, a *draugr!* Inside, he longed for a simple life as a farmer like his father. One last man needed to fall.

A flicker of red caught his eye and Brand saw the strangest bird he had ever seen. It was all red like a glowing coal with a crest of feathers on its head. It sat and watched Brand with red eyes before opening its beak to warble. Then it flew off. Immediately, Brand thought of Runa. She was like the red bird, rare and beautiful and he took it as a positive sign. When this day was over, he would take Runa away and they would begin a new life together. Her sweet spirit would help mend his brokenness and he would rescue her from the cruelty of her life. As soon as he killed Eiland Biersson, who had been his *friend.*

Brand strapped on his armor and tested his blade by throwing an oak leaf into the air and slicing it in two. The sundered leaf halves fell to the ground with a whisper. His blade was as sharp as a shaving knife, and it was finally time. He turned and headed toward the village of Lyngmarker. Beside him, he felt the ghosts of his family watching and protecting him. Eiland was at Gorm's hall, and Brand would find him there, call him out and the battle would ensue. Brand's debt would be paid before the sun reached the middle of the sky.

His boots crunched through the leaves and detritus of the forest floor, but all around him was quiet. The feast drums were silent and the shouts of people celebrating and children playing were gone. The land held its breath while death stalked toward the village and death's name was Brand Keitelsson. Though only one man would die today, and that man's name was Eiland Biersson. Vengeance would no longer be denied.

Leaving the path and entering the clearing to the longhouse, Brand was shocked at the sight that met his eyes. The entire village had gathered to watch the battle. Many thanes, fully armed and dangerous, stood as a barrier to the main hall. As he looked toward the massive building that had been Eiland's hiding place for twelve long days, rage filled him.

Gorm had a different plan for the day after the solstice and it would begin with Runa. He would punish her for her insolence and shame her in front of everyone. He would strip her bare and lash her until he no longer craved her. Vidar would be there to kill the stranger and the fight with the old man would not take place. Then he would banish Eiland Biersson, and the girl and his enemy's bastard would be out of Gorm's life forever and the lust for his wife's daughter would stop torturing him.

Runa had been tied between two pillars with her arms outstretched. Her dress had been torn down the back exposing the soft pink flesh of her back. Vidar stood by slowly swinging a long leather whip. It was obvious what he intended.

When he saw Runa, the red mist took over Brand's sight and he shook his head trying to think clearly. What was the meaning of all this? He drew his sword and pointed it toward Gorm.

"The solstice celebration is over! Release Runa she has no part in this! Send out the old man. You gave your oath in front of all these people." Brand commanded Gorm who stood smugly on the stairs leading to his longhouse.

"You have not acted in good faith Brand Keitelsson, and so I am changing the agreement."

"How have I not acted in good faith?" Brand yelled in astonishment. "I waited twelve long days to fight my enemy as we agreed. That was my only part of the *heitstrenging*. Your wife poisoned me, your son tried to wound me so that I could not fight. You are an oath breaker and have not kept your word, Gorm Haaglanden! You are a man without honor and a coward!"

Before Gorm could answer, the doors of the great hall opened and out came Eiland Biersson. He staggered forward covered in a tattered blanket, bent over, and leaning on a staff, but when he saw what was going on, he threw the blanket off and stood tall. He was bare to the waist with his long sword sheathed at his side and looked like Odin himself come to battle.

"What is the meaning of this Gorm? Release Runa! She is innocent of any wrongdoing!" Eiland was astonished at the number of men surrounding Brand Keitelsson and at Runa's state. He stormed forward drawing his sword to cut Runa's bonds, but he was blocked by four men who grabbed his arms and dragged him into the center courtyard beside Brand.

Brand had his enemy standing before him, but the woman he loved was in danger. Now they would face off. He was ready to fight, but Eiland was looking at Runa and took a step toward her. Brand would not strike if his opponent's back was turned toward him. He wanted to see the light of life fade from his eyes, but not like this. Instead, Brand stepped forward to stand side-by-side with his enemy.

"Release the girl!" Eiland shouted in a strong voice. Gorm only grinned back at him.

Something in the crowd shifted and behind them, came Flynn Bloodhead with his men. Flynn's men formed a line behind Brand and Eiland.

"Gorm Haaglanden is an oath breaker! We all heard him give his promise to Brand Keitelsson. He promised Brand would collect his blood debt at the end of the solstice festival. Now he goes back on his word. I say no true leader, no good Jarl would break his word. He tortures the daughter he claims as his and stands as a traitor to the people by his actions! I claim the right of challenge to right these wrongs!"

"You interfere with things you know nothing of. It is my right to discipline a disobedient daughter as I see fit. I am your Jarl, through appointment by the king who appointed my father before me and his father before him! Even if you win the challenge my son would be Jarl, not you, Flynn Bloodhead!"

"I claim the right of arms! You have acted dishonorably and now you balk like a coward. I say it is time for a new Jarl who will act with honor and fairness. Fight me or forever be branded as a lying coward!"

"Let Runa go!" Eiland shouted in the argument.

"Fight if you will, but let Runa go, she is innocent and has nothing to do with any of this!" Brand shouted.

"Innocent, is she?" Gorm hollered above the stirring voices in the crowd. "Some innocent! She lays with you in the forest and then seeks the bed of your enemy, Eiland Biersson. She is nothing but a Hóra who gives herself to any man who asks."

Brand staggered back as if he had just been struck. Had Runa given herself to his enemy? The berserker clawed inside his skull to get free, and his eyes burned red with fury. How could he stand knowing that the woman he loved had lain with his greatest enemy? He stared where she hung with her head bent down in shame. The long red locks covered her face and Brand could not see her eyes. Then the voice of his enemy shouted above the buzzing rage in his head.

"He lies!" Eiland cried out. "I've been too ill to take any woman to bed. You all have seen!" Eiland swept an arm around gesturing at the people. "Gorm has no proof to back such a claim!"

"I saw it with my own eyes! Her! In the forest with Brand Keitelsson and then with Eiland Biersson in the bathhouse. She gave herself to that old man! To both men!" Gorm cried.

"You've no second witness to corroborate what you say. I say you lie for your own gain." Flynn Bloodhead strode forward.

The people stirred and looked back and forth between Gorm and Flynn.

"You men squabble like gossiping women!" A new voice rose from the crowd.

Signe pushed her way forward and strode toward the longhouse steps where her husband stood. She was golden in the morning light with her back straight and her chin held high.

"You disgrace both houses by your actions, all of you! I command you to break this up immediately and go home! You're still drunk from celebrating the solstice. Cool your heads and go your separate ways, there will be no right of arms, no challenge, and displacement of the jarldom. Gorm is the ruler here and Vidar, *my son*, will be afterward. It is the way it has always been done." Pointing to Runa, Signe commanded. "Vidar cut her down!"

Vidar looked to Gorm who looked at him, Runa, and Signe. Then he nodded once and cut Runa down. She collapsed on the steps of the longhouse cradling her hands in her lap before untying the ropes from her wrists. Then holding her dress up to cover herself, she jumped up and pushed through the line of Gorm's men to go stand between Brand and Eiland.

Flynn took charge. "I say there is a challenge not answered. Fight me Gorm, for the jarldom. I will claim the right to rule Lyngmarker by right of victory in battle!"

Gorm had enough, he drew his sword and charged forward, his sons and his men followed. Right in the middle were Brand, Runa, and Eiland. Behind them, Flynn and his men let loose their battle cries and they charged as well.

Eiland pushed Runa out of the way of a descending sword, right into Brand's arms. Then he whirled and engaged with one of the thanes.

"Run Brand! Take Runa and go!" Eiland shouted at Brand over his shoulder then turned toward the charging warriors to defend their backs.

Chapter Twenty-four

Brand did not know what to do, but his protective instincts kicked in and he grabbed Runa's hand before turning to run toward the main gates surrounding the village. The clash of swords and the shouting of battle cries rang out as men who had drank and celebrated together the day before, now fought each other to the death. Gorm and Flynn clashed hacking and doing their best to kill each other. Signe was screaming at them all to stop and Eiland was protecting Brand's back.

Runa looked back to see the old warrior swinging his sword with great skill and she feared for his life. The number of men against him was too great.

"Brand! We can't just leave him!" she tried to reason with him.

The red mist of fury was clouding Brand's mind and he desperately wanted to go back and fight his enemy, but through the confusion of his thoughts and his heart's desire, he heard Runa's voice pleading with him.

"Go!" Brand shoved her toward the gates. He turned back and ran toward Eiland's back with his sword raised. Runa could not look.

Eiland was fighting two men at once while all around him the chaos of battle grew. Flynn's men were attacking Gorm's men, and the screams of the dying rose into the sky calling the Valkyries. Blocking a vicious blow by a man he had shared a mead horn with the previous day, Eiland did not see a sword swiping down toward his head on the other side. He would not be fast enough to avoid it and, turning, he saw and knew that this was the end.

The strike did not come. A sword came from his left and blocked the killing blow. The man who held the defending sword was Brand Keitelsson. They fought side by side, backing slowly away toward the gates to escape. Guards from atop the walls were running in to join the battle and Eiland and Brand managed to turn and run. The war being fought here was not their fight and they cared not who prevailed.

When Runa saw Brand and Eiland running toward her, she waited for them and then turned to run as soon as they were beside her. She led them toward the fields of heather. Reaching the far-off spot where she hid the supplies, she stopped to catch her breath. Eiland and Brand were seconds behind. Each of them was blood splattered and out of breath. Brand had a cut on his cheek and Eiland's neck had been nicked, but they were alive. The blood splattering them was not their own.

Runa looked at both of the men she loved. The wind whispered to her and revealed that there was no resolution to be had between the three of them. Ignorance and greed won back in Lyngmarker, but there was so much more between her and the two men she loved. Overhead a crow cawed in the blue sky.

"It is true?" Brand shouted as he whirled toward Runa. "You laid with my enemy?"

Runa parted her lips to tell him the truth, but Eiland spoke before she could.

"NO!" Eiland lied to Brand, but held Runa's gaze, entreating her to be silent. "Runa is innocent. I never touched her. Gorm lied for his own gain and to put you out of your head before the fight. You witnessed, he is an oath-breaker and a deceiver, and not to be trusted. Do not blame Runa for any of this."

Brand stared at Eiland and something inside him knew the old man lied. He turned to look at Runa and saw her turn her head and look at him. Understanding passed between them and he knew the truth, but the love in her eyes touched his heart and he felt his anger toward her slowly dying, just as Eiland's next words broke the silence between them.

"Come, sword brother," Eiland gestured with his sword and struck himself in the chest. The show of strength was a challenge. "Let us end this. A fight to the death is all that is left between us. I expect no quarter because I'll give none, but if I should be the one to fall, promise me you will take Runa, make her your wife, and love her until the end of your days."

"Brand," Runa stepped between them, "You always have a choice. Let there be an end to hatred and vengeance. Let Eiland live. You do not have to fight."

Brand stared at her and slowly lowered his sword tip. Runa was about to breathe a sigh of relief thinking he would relent, but Eiland spoke first.

"But *I* do." Eiland's voice was hard as he gently pulled Runa out of the way, putting her behind him. "You have hunted me like an animal for ten long years, *draugr*. You killed my thanes and took everything I had and denied me the life I should have had. I have a choice as well and I choose to fight you. Raise your sword, boy, we fight to the death!"

Chapter Twenty-five

Runa whispered a pleading, *"No"* as Eiland stepped to the side, drawing Brand away to keep her safe from the swinging swords. Brand raised his sword and took a deep breath. Eiland lunged forward. Around them, the heather swayed unaffected as the two warriors met with a clash of swords.

Brand blocked a killing blow and retaliated. Eiland was winded from the battle and the run. He staggered back, feeling in his bones all fifty of the winters he had been on the earth. Brand was swinging at his head again and they traded bone-crushing blows. The clang of metal upon metal rang across the heather fields as the final battle between the two enemies finally proceeded.

The stench of blood and sweat rose over the scent of the heather crushed beneath the two men's boots. Brand fought with the strength and fury of a berserker and Eiland fought with calm intensity. He beat back Brand's sword trading blows, dodging thrusts, and retaliating blow for blow. It looked like they were equally matched, but Eiland was older, and he began to show signs of slowing. His blocks grew clumsy, and Brand knew he had him. He gave a thought to ending the fight with a draw, but then Eiland swung toward his neck and barely missed separating his head from his shoulders.

Leaning back, Brand missed what would have been a decapitating strike. Whirling around and gathering momentum, biceps rippling, both legs propelled him into a leap, his sword went up and came crashing down between Eiland's shoulder and neck. The crunching sound of breaking bone and a harsh whoosh of breath testified to the strength of the blow. Brand drew his sword down his enemy's shattered chest and cut a thick line of blood through his skin. Eiland staggered back mortally wounded and fell back into the heather, his sword clenched tightly in his hand.

Runa screamed and ran past where Brand stood breathing hard, shaking the blood mist from his mind, and blinking to clear his eyesight of the berserker fury. He looked down to see Runa kneeling by Eiland's side, holding his hand to her breast. As clarity came back to him, he realized that his last enemy lay dying at his feet, and he felt...*nothing*. No sense of justice, no feeling of elation that he had succeeded came. He just felt empty. The blood debt was finally fully paid, but his friend lay gasping out his last breaths and the only woman he ever loved, wept by his side.

Brand sheathed his sword and knelt on Eiland's other side. Reaching for his bloody hand still clenching his sword, he gently pulled the sword free and joined their hands. Runa was leaning over him. She whispered something in Eiland's ear, and he smiled at her through bloody teeth. Raising their hands over his ruined chest,

Eiland brought Brand's hand to Runa's and clasped them together with the last of his strength. He looked Brand in the eye and gasped.

"Promise, take care of her. Give your oath!"

"I give you my oath," Brand promised and stood.

Now that Runa's safety was secured, Eiland turned his head and pulled her down to whisper his last words to her alone. Runa nodded, whispered something back, and kissed him as his last breath passed through his lips and life faded from his eyes.

Brand let Runa cry and remembered what she said, he had choices and she had choices. Maybe he made bad choices and maybe not, but he had chosen the honorable path. The blood quest was fulfilled, his family was avenged, and their spirits could now rest. There was one more choice left to make. He reached down and pulled Runa to her feet. He wrapped his arms around her, holding tightly until she had no more tears to spill.

"Let us shed no more tears for him." Finally, Brand spoke gently, "Even though he was my enemy, I say Eiland Biersson died honorably. He went out fighting with his sword in his hand and Valhalla will welcome him." They turned to go. "Come, it is time to go home."

In the distance, the sounds of battle died, and the cries of grieving women rose on the wind. Shouts of,

"Bloodhead! Bloodhead!" rang out in victory, but he did not care. He turned and picked up Eiland's sword and picked up his own. Then he grabbed the bags that Runa hid in the heather. He took her hand, and they both stared down at Eiland's body.

Clouds passed over the sun and the wind buffeted them whipping up dirt and shaking the heather around them. The shadowy form of a woman on horseback materialized above them and descended from the sky to land beside Eiland. The horse stamped silver hooves and the woman's golden armor was a blinding flash in the sunlight. Brand and Runa watched as the Valkyrie held a hand out to Eiland. Glowing with a white light he rose, took her hand and they mounted together riding away on the white horse that climbed into the sky before disappearing into the clouds.

Chapter Twenty-six

Runa and Brand walked until night fell and it was too dark to see. They made camp and he wrapped her in his arms, and they fell fast asleep. In the following days and months, they made their way through mountains and fields until they came to a small town called Kysten Sid, on the shores of Norway. They made plans to earn money to buy a small boat and head north toward the Jutland peninsula where Brand's home lay in burned ruin.

When Runa missed her moon cycle, she knew that she was pregnant, and the knowledge was heavy on her heart. So, she told him the truth one night while they lay under the stars with the sound of the sea waves gently strumming the sandy shore.

She confessed everything including that Eiland had lied on her behalf so that Brand would never know that she and Eiland had been lovers. Then she told him she was pregnant and that she had no way of knowing if the child, conceived during the solstice festival, was Brand's or Eiland's.

This information was not a surprise to Brand as he had known Eiland lied but was so moved by his love for Runa that he forgave his old friend, and her, almost immediately. The last fight had been a surprise to Brand as his hatred had been doused by Runa's words. He did realize he had a choice not to kill his friend and was willing to let his final revenge go until Eiland forced the fight. Now with the friend gone, he regretted the way it all turned out, but with Runa by his side, the path ahead led to forgiveness and healing.

"What did he say to you before he died?" Brand asked.

"Eiland said he loved me. He said...he had to fight you because you both could not have me and so he let fate decide."

#

The months passed and Runa grew large with the pregnancy and one day, two months before the solstice festival, she gave birth to two boys. They were twins, but not identical. One boy was golden-haired and the other had a shock of red hair just like Runa's. Their joy was complete and with every solstice, they celebrated their love and the peace of the life they built together.

Epilogue

Brand sailed his small boat loaded with provisions, tools, and his family. Two three-year-old boys leaned over the bow of the boat and stared into the water. They laughed and pretended to see silvery fish following along under the water. Runa sat dozing in the sun. She was heavy with their third child.

When they reached the shores of the Jutland peninsula, Brand lifted each boy out and set them in the sand. They quickly ran off to play. Helping Runa down, he placed a kiss on her forehead.

"Are you alright?" Brand asked.

"I am, but just a little achy and tired." She smiled and arched her back.

"This one is a girl. I know it!" Brand grinned.

Turning back to the boat. He lifted a long-wrapped bundle and handed it to Runa. Then he grabbed bags of provisions to carry up to the house he had been building for the last few years. Runa slowly made her way up the path with the long bundle.

From up the shore, the little red-headed boy came racing back to her side.

"Mama! I have to go!" he danced from foot to foot.

"Go up in the bushes just there. I'll wait for you. Go on."

The little boy ran a few steps away and hurried to pull down his britches to relieve himself. Runa watched as a patch of her son's skin was revealed. She stared at the oak leaf birthmark low on his hip and gave a sad smile. Unwrapping the end of the bundle she held, she stared at the hilt of Eiland's sword with a flush of sadness.

The boy finished, hiked up his pants, and ran off, but stopped at the top of the hill to yell back at her.

"Hurry Mama!"

"I'm coming, Eiland!"

Runa covered the sword hilt and started up the hill again. She looked around at the beautiful land that was her new home, as wonder and elation threatened to make her cry. Her other son appeared by her side and looked up at her with Brand's distinct features and ice-blue eyes. She did not know how the goddess did it, but somehow Runa knew that one of her sons was Brand's and the other was Eiland's. The wind picked up and Runa heard the goddess's voice speaking in her mind.

"Do not lament, Solstice Child, I determine the path these brothers will walk."

Her daughter kicked inside her womb and her belly contracted with pain. Runa bent over and breathed deeply until the pain subsided. Warm water flowed down her legs as her water broke. A burst of fear flooded her, surely it was too soon. It could not be time yet. She mentally counted the months back and tried to figure out when she and Brand conceived their daughter. She stopped, realizing it must have been at the last solstice celebration. Runa looked up as Brand walked toward her and she understood. She carried another solstice child.

For another Viking fantasy romance by Wendy L. Anderson, click on the link and read about twin sisters who fight to find happiness in a ruthless world ruled by the sword and axe!

A Cut Twice as Deep

by Wendy L. Anderson

Thank you for reading Solstice Child, a Viking fantasy romance. I sincerely hope you enjoyed reading it as much as I enjoyed writing it.

You can help other readers fall in love with my fantasy books by leaving a review. It helps greatly. Remember, a review doesn't have to be lengthy or complicated, just...Keep-It-Simple-Sweet-Reader!

Keep in touch with me for information on writing and updates on new books by subscribing to my newsletter. Just click here and sign up now!

Thank you for your support in reading my books. I wish you endless blessings and happy reading.

You can find out more about me and all of my books on my website:

https://www.wendylanderson.com

Also, from this author:

The Kingdom of Jior Epic Fantasy Romance Series

Of Demon Kind, book one
Redemption of the Fallen, book two
Heirs of Jior, book three
Iron and the Arrow, book four
The Last Ny-Failen, book five

and
My spin-off fantasy series, the Legends of
Everclearing

If you're more into stand-alone books, try one of these fabulous fantasies.

Ulrik is a time travel fantasy romance full of heart-stopping action!
Rapunzel's Tower is a fractured fairy tale that will sweep you away!

Don't forget…share your love of reading. Post a review!

Printed in Great Britain
by Amazon

52943491R00136